FIRST TO LIE

UNRAVELED BOOK 1

MARIE JOHNSTON

LE PUBLISHING

First to Lie

Copyright 2017 as Unmistaken Identity by Marie Johnston

Developmental Editing by The Killion Group

Copy Editing by Razor Sharp Editing

Cover Art by Secret Identity Graphics

Second edition proofing by My Brother's Editor and Double Author Services

The characters, places, and events in this story are fictional. Any similarities to real people, places, or events are coincidental and unintentional.

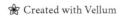 Created with Vellum

CHAPTER 1

ara

I STRODE into the swanky club and stalled. Loud music pulsed through my body and flashing lights bounced off mirrored columns. Beautiful people sipped cocktails and flirted with the equally stunning people next to them.

I so didn't belong there.

Sam, why'd you have to go and die on me? Guilt immediately poured in. It wasn't like the man I leased my storefront from, my dear friend, had planned on passing away.

To fortify my nerves, I reminded myself why I was here instead of at home in my *Avengers* pajamas, slaying some dragon ass on Xbox. Per the notice, I only had forty-five days to close down my comic book shop and vacate the building. The entire strip mall was scheduled for demolition.

Sam Robson's son must've moved on his plans to tear down my livelihood before dirt had even covered the coffin.

I smoothed my hands down my skirt and wished for my

favorite Wonder Woman leggings and plaid flannel. My feet screamed in these heels, but at least I shouldn't get kicked out for being an ugly duckling in a sea of sleek, designer label-wearing swans.

Why couldn't Sam's son have met with me like a responsible business owner? Why couldn't Sam have finished the paperwork that would've taken care of everything and given me the building?

I'm sorry, Mr. Robson isn't in the office today.

Wesley Robson's bitchy receptionist had said that line for the last five days. First, the coward had served me papers on *Friday* afternoon, then he'd been "gone" all week. If he thought to avoid me, he was an idiot. I'd meet his unprofessionalism with my tenacity. To start with, I'd remembered Sam telling me his son owned a nightclub.

And here I was. At Canon. Of all the definitions of canon, which one had he named his club after? I doubted he used religious connotations in the name of a nightclub. In my world, canon discussions varied depending on the universe being discussed. Comic books? Superhero movies? Video games? Yeah, those worlds totally went with this swanky place…

I glanced around at the design and decor of the club. Upscale. Like the high-end retail shopping and luxury condos planned for where my store sat. What was this look called? Industrial contemporary. Another term I'd heard Sam throw around. I'd learned so much from that man.

Six months of mourning his death gave way to a spike in anger. He'd told me he'd take care of it, that my business would never be threatened. The papers that gave me the Heart of Downtown strip mall had been drawn up and…that was as far as it had gotten. He had loved my comic book shop, Arcadia, almost as much as I did.

Squaring my shoulders, I forced one foot in front of the

other. As I passed the bouncer, he slid his gaze down my bare legs, up to my plunging neckline, then behind me to the next scantily clad woman. He had plenty to choose from, and, as always, I was forgettable.

I sighed. No wonder the fanboy world was where I stayed. Most days, comic book worlds were preferable to mine, and my customers brightened each hour I worked. Hell, they were my only friends.

I scanned the club as I wound my way around mirrored columns to the bar. Throngs of young professionals left their business jackets behind and bounced in beat to the music, their ties loose and neck collars unbuttoned. Dark booths lining the walls—I was almost afraid to look—were filled with laughing men and women, elegant drinks in their hands. As the night progressed, I was sure the activities in those booths would get more salacious.

The bar anchored the middle of the club and I chose a seat on the same side as the door. A prime view of every corner.

The bartender gave me a once-over. "What can I get you?"

"I'd like to talk to Wes if he's around." Maybe acting like I knew him would help. But what if he went by Wesley?

The guy cocked an eyebrow. "He's not here."

A ready-made answer. A lot of women must make the same request. Perfect. The guy was a player. At least that might mean he harvested his bedroom fun from the dance floor and would make an appearance.

Ugh. I hated lingering at bars.

What the hell did people drink when they went to places like this? Mixed drinks? I didn't know any. Beer? I liked it with pizza. "I'll have a glass of white wine."

There. That sounded classy.

He rattled off a list of brands, his tone bored.

I gave him a succinct smile. "Surprise me."

He poured my wine as he made a phone call. My lips flattened when I noticed he'd chosen bottom shelf. Was I that obvious? I wasn't penniless, but I did pinch the copper out of them.

He slid the glass in front of me and moved down the line, taking orders.

Sipping my drink and watching the crowd, I waffled between ordering a second glass and going home. Could I tolerate sitting at the bar, wasting time, while my mind vacillated between finding another location for my store and giving it up to work for someone else?

I shuddered. Giving someone power and influence over me?

Not again.

I had to hunt Wesley Robson down tonight, didn't want to waste more time on my search. As it was, the night would be too short for a decent sleep. Saturday was game day at my comic book shop. Participants showed early and played intensely for hours. Board games, card games, electronic games. I would jump in and play them all, or run around the store helping customers.

It was my favorite day of the week, but still a long one.

What did Wesley look like, anyway? I would've seen him if I'd been able to go to the funeral. By the time I'd found out about Sam's sudden death, though, he'd been gone and buried. There had to be a picture of his boy online. Just as I pulled out my phone to do a search, someone settled onto the barstool next to me.

"Macallan 18."

The deep voice resonated through my bones. I almost groaned. He had the rumble of a rugged man, a primal mating call in my opinion. Admittedly, my last few dates had put the "boys" in fanboys, not men who knew their way around a woman.

I peeked at him from the corner of my eye. My fingers tightened around the stem of my glass.

Holy hotness, Batman! He reminded me of one of my favorite superheroes. Jet-black hair, sky-blue eyes nearly glowing under the club lights, wide shoulders. If he wore a cape and had a large S on his shirt, I'd sit on his face. I'd still consider it, given his charcoal slacks and white-striped shirt, which likely had been cinched by a tie all day. The first two buttons were undone and his sleeves were rolled up. What was that style called? Industrial hot-as-hell businessman.

"What's your poison?"

I shot him a surprised glance. He gestured to my already half-empty glass.

What had the bartender said it was? "I think it's named after some pop star."

He chuckled with genuine humor. "Are you here with the bachelorette party?"

When hell froze over. "No."

The bartender leaned over the counter to hand him his drink. "The lady said she was looking for the owner."

Stay out of it, dude. Wait, he knew the total package next to me? Maybe the new arrival also knew the owner. "Do you know Mr. Robson?"

His eyes crinkled with his smile. Even the man's teeth were perfect. "Why would you want to find him? I've heard he's an ass."

I rolled my eyes. "Tell me about it."

Hotness savored a long sip of his...whatever a Macallan was. "You've gotta tell me what he did to you."

The pink bangs that framed my face dropped into my eyes. I feathered them away. His gaze traced from my hand to my dual ponytails, the plain brown hair streaked with pink. Instead of blond highlights, or lowlights, or whatever stylish women did, I'd chosen pink—because it was fun and girly. One of the few splurges I allowed myself.

My hair often drew attention, not always the flattering kind. But I enjoyed his. "He's shutting down my store. Tearing down the whole damn building. 'Upgrading.'" I gave the last word air quotes.

His right eye twitched and he stared at me for a heartbeat. Humor drained from his expression and his gaze narrowed slightly.

My heart rate increased at being the object of such scrutiny. I wanted more, but I also felt like I'd done something wrong.

Finally, a grin curled his full lips. "That bastard." He flagged the bartender. "The lady would like another glass."

If he was going to sit next to me, then yes, I would like another glass. Unless he wanted to do more than sit. Because getting it on with a sexy stranger would take the sting out of having to purchase this outfit just to get close to Wesley-fucking-Robson.

But first, the standard wedding ring check. Not always a reliable sign, but the tan line of a missing ring cut things off immediately.

His left hand was wrapped around the wide glass of his whiskey. No white line.

Good start.

He turned to me. "The name's Sam."

"Mara. I lost a good friend named Sam." *Way to go. A hot guy starts talking to you and you bring up your dead friend.*

An unreadable expression flickered over his face. "I'm sorry to hear that." He paused and his expression lightened. "Closing your store, huh?"

I swiveled in my seat. The position landed my crossed legs between his manspread. An intimate position, and not one I wanted to leave. "Yeah, my store. I was good friends with this amazing man who supported my business and gave me sound investment advice. He's who I leased the building from." I blinked back the sting of tears. "But his son is tearing it all down and throwing up some…" I couldn't come up with any words that weren't foul, so I went with it. "Fancy shit."

The corner of his mouth lifted, and holy X-wing, had his eyes just sparkled? "Is that the technical term?"

"I'm the wrong person to ask." I waved my hand at the crowd on the dance floor. "You'd have to ask one of them."

His expression danced with amusement. "Not your crowd, I take it."

"God, no." I shook my head, my ponytails swinging. "I'm sorry, I don't mean to be insulting. I had to grow up fast and it didn't leave me time for any of this."

The scorching heat in his gaze as it wandered down my body and back up robbed me of breath. His attention didn't switch to another woman, like the bouncer's had. Blatant interest was written all over his face. I took a gulp of my fresh glass of wine.

His hand brushed my leg. "If it's not your crowd, why don't we go someplace else?" His gaze held mine as he took another sip.

Yes, please! My shoulders hunched. "Sorry, I'm on asshole patrol."

Sam almost spit his drink back out. He swallowed hard and chuckled. "Well then. Let's hit the dance floor and watch for assholes."

Before I lost my nerve, I drained the rest of my wine and hopped up. The world spun off-kilter. A strong hand steadied me at my waist.

I held my hand to my forehead. "I think I might have to take you up on that offer and use it to go grab a bite."

He frowned, his eyes glimmering. "You were drinking on an empty stomach?"

I smiled ruefully and leaned into the hand at my hip. "Not every decision I make is excellent." Though usually it had to be, and it was *exhausting*. Tonight, I wanted him to be my one rash decision. If I had to waste time and money at this damn club, I wanted compensation.

He dropped his head to speak into my ear, his breath sending delicious shivers down my spine. "Staying to dance with me is a good one. I promise I'll feed you soon."

My breath caught. We were both on the same page: take advantage of our mutual attraction and act on it without any inhibitions. Years of responsibility melted away. It wasn't like I was looking for a relationship. As long as he didn't have a wife or girlfriend waiting on him somewhere, I could handle it. Death by guilt wasn't for me.

Why shouldn't I relish the attention of a hot guy? Letting myself go for one night wouldn't hurt.

∼

Wes

My erection ground into Mara's back as she swayed against me. Her claims of being an awkward dancer were only slightly true, but that might be the effect of the wine.

Mara Jade Baranski.

I didn't trust her as far as I could throw her. Maybe even that would be too far. She was a foot shorter than me and weighed maybe 120 pounds; I could toss her a ways. I couldn't come up with another euphemism because her scent was too distracting. Her hair smelled like it looked—strawberries.

Asshole patrol. Everything she said had been accurate. One day, I would tell her it was deliberate and why, how she couldn't use her looks to cruise through life on the backs of hardworking men. She could take her little shop and move it to a shittier part of Minneapolis, where no horny old man would help her.

Like every other time I thought of my dad, my heart wrenched and I brushed it off.

When my bartender had rung me in the office to say a woman was asking about me, I'd pulled up the security footage on my computer. She was *smokin'*—and unfamiliar, but that was unsurprising. She was just another woman with ulterior motives for a man with money. Shocker. But her appearance had been worth a look-see. Then to discover it was *her*; she'd upped her ante from stopping by my office. From the way her body felt against mine, it'd be worth indulging a little while I fooled her with my dad's name.

The corner of my mouth tilted. The irony. She'd tried to scam my dad, so "Sam" would scam her. My dad and I had issues, and some days, I would love to know where they stemmed from, but I wouldn't allow Mara to stomp on his memory.

I flared my hands at her hips and pulled her closer to nibble along her neck. She arched into me. Women weren't welcome at my home or any of my offices—I didn't trust a girl not to be after my money, and none of those locales would do because Mara would find out who I really was before I could uncover why she'd targeted my dad. What did Mara have that Sam's other women hadn't? As far as I knew, Sam had never entertained the thought of even remarrying, much less signing over property for as little as a *dollar*.

Mara wasn't like any of the flings my dad had brought around. She looked barely out of college, but she was just a few years younger than my twenty-eight.

Not surprising why good ol' Sam had never told me about her. Sam had kept the hot girl to himself, perhaps fearing that given his age, she would have set her sights on me instead.

What had my dad been thinking, drooling after a younger woman?

I dragged my tongue up to her earlobe and reveled in her shiver. "Gimme your keys and tell me where to go."

Her dreamy gaze locked on me. She licked her lips, catching my attention. I couldn't help the rock of my hips to ease the throbbing in my balls.

"I came here to—" She moaned when I nibbled a path down to the juncture of her neck and collarbone. Warm and salty, hinting at the sweetness I hoped to discover between her thighs.

"If he was going to show, he'd be here by now. Besides," I nipped her soft skin, "there's always another night."

She caught her lower lip between her teeth. No big surprise she was going to acquiesce. Mara had proven with my dad how quickly she could sink her unadorned nails into a man. Only I wasn't going to sign over part of my empire to her just because she had an epic ass.

"Come on." She grasped my hand and we wove through the crowd until we exited into the crisp night air.

We reached her car and she stumbled in her heels. I caught her and pulled her in close. No wonder my impulsive dad had been smitten. Mara rated even higher than any of the women I had dated. Well, "dated" was a strong word.

I dropped my head and captured her mouth. Plump and soft, I had to taste. Sweeping my tongue inside, I thumbed a nipple through her shirt.

She groaned a sigh, such a feminine sound, and I wanted her to make it repeatedly.

Lost in pleasure, I let my tongue dance with hers before I realized we were rubbing against each other. If I had to wait until we got to her place, I was going to lose my mind to my blue balls.

A peculiar need rode me. Like one night might not be enough. Perhaps it was knowing she'd curse and despise me later, and I wanted to play as long as I could.

I broke away to take her keys. After I settled a flushed Mara into the passenger seat, I jogged around to the driver's side and moved the seat back so I could fold my frame inside.

Mara's hand was on her lips like she couldn't believe the wattage of that kiss. I'd admit, she would receive a gold star for kissing.

"Was that the appetizer?" Her luminous eyes reflected the city lights.

I ignored the tightening in my gut at her guileless expression. She was a con artist and I planned to con the con. She had targeted an old man with a bad heart, and maybe she'd slept with him, maybe she'd strung him along. It didn't matter. I wasn't worried about being compared to anyone, much less my father. We'd been nothing more than colleagues since I was a teenager. It'd been years since I'd felt like I even had a dad.

Shoving those thoughts away, I flipped the car into drive. "Where we going?"

CHAPTER 2

es

She rattled off her address. I thought my father would've set her up in better accommodations. It was in an older part of town. Not dangerous, but quaint.

Thinking of Sam with her, I put more pressure on the gas. It should be a turn-off, but she was so *adorable*. Is that how she'd done it? And how many other men had handed over money and property they'd worked hard for? Sam had literally worked himself to death.

I would make sure she knew what it felt like, give her a taste of how a duplicitous relationship felt.

"Whoa, Ensign." She peered over her shoulder. "Ease up on the warp speed. Getting pulled over will only delay us and I want to see what you've got."

Her statement alone had me slowing down. A chuckle slipped out. "What did you just say?"

Her grin was pure wickedness, her eyes flashing with

mirth. "My store is a comic book and gaming shop, didn't I mention that?"

"F'real?" I feigned surprise. "So you're all up on your Star Trek knowledge?"

She tilted her head, her gaze speculative. "I'm not the only one."

My grin faded. "I'm a nineties kid. Of course, I've watched the series."

"Oh, I see." She folded her arms across her chest, a smile playing over her lips. "You go to a swanky club, dress sharp, so it's not cool to display your inner fanboy?"

Actually, that was really accurate. "Nailed it."

She leaned close and whispered into my ear, sending shivers straight to my painfully hard cock. "Once I'm done with you, you'll be screaming for me to beam you up and begging me to wield your lightsaber."

My brows shot up and my foot twitched to stomp on the gas. "I'm going to test you on that."

"Oh, right here." She pointed to a small house that wasn't any larger than my walk-in closet.

Like the other tiny, square houses on the block, hers had peeling, powder-blue Masonite siding. I'd call the dwelling and its yard tidy but not something she made a priority.

"Ignore the seventies chic. I'm going to paint it next summer if I have the time or money." She climbed out of the car muttering, "I can't seem to have both at the same time."

"You live here alone?" I didn't know why I'd asked. She'd hardly keep someone under the same roof while playing my dad.

"My mom moved out last year." She trotted to the door, but her voice didn't match the bounce in her step.

Her tone seemed melancholy as she spoke of her mom, whereas mine would have been resentful if I'd talked about my mother.

She let me in with a promising smile. I'd have taken her against the door, but the decor stalled me as soon as I entered.

Scanning the room, I didn't know where to look first. Every time I spotted something of interest, another bauble caught my eye. "You have the whole Star Trek crew in action figures?"

"You'll have to be more specific." She laughed and shut the door. "I just got the remake's crew. Can't go wrong with the latest Captain Kirk."

My gaze swung to the coffee table stretching in front of a threadbare couch. On it was a line-up of familiar characters wearing black pants and a mix of red-and-gold shirts with com badges. "I haven't seen the new movies."

The action figures coaxed unwanted memories to the surface. Sam's broad smile as he brandished a two-foot replica of the *Enterprise*. Binge-watching whole seasons on the weekends. Making each other laugh by talking like Captain Kirk. I stuffed them back down. Figured Sam would turn his fanboy tendencies on a woman when he'd left me behind at warp speed after the divorce.

"Seriously?" She stepped out of her shoes and the flash of leg was enough to tear my gaze off her toys. "I have old Spock, new Spock. Old Kirk, new Kirk. They picked excellent actors for the remake, in my opinion."

With her heels off, she was even shorter. Not quite petite, but a perfect size to lift and thrust into. As I examined her toys, my mind surprisingly turned away from sex.

"Maybe I'll watch them sometime." With Sam gone, would I still have the same animosity toward films we'd used to enjoy together? Nothing Trek had graced my screens since the turn of the century.

She closed the distance between us. "What about the new

Star Wars? You had to have seen that? I think everyone in the world has."

Star Wars. I clenched my jaw but forced myself to relax. "I saw *Episode I* with my dad." The next episode I'd seen by myself...because Sam had decided spending time with me was a waste of time. Said those very words after I had called, asking why he hadn't shown. Getting sent to an out-of-state boarding school had almost been a relief.

By *Episode III*, I'd given up on the things that'd bonded me with Sam and concentrated on college. It's not like I hadn't known who Anakin would turn out to be.

Her hands skimmed up my shirt front and stopped at the top button. My mind embraced sex again. She pulled in her lower lip to chew. A nervous habit, or meant to be provocative? I'd never seen a girl do that, but then they usually had so much shellac on their lips it stained their teeth. It was hard enough scrubbing the stuff off my skin, and I'd heard the housekeeper's curses about bleaching red tint out of my collars. Or waistbands.

I waited for her to undo each button, then tugged on a ponytail, earning a flush from her. "I'm going to keep your skirt on when I fuck you."

Pupils dilated. She liked that idea, and how I said it.

"I was expecting a crappy night." She dragged his shirt out of his waistband, slipped each button free. "I thought I'd be so steaming angry that I'd turn into She-Hulk."

Her touch drove me into a single-minded spiral of need. The extra layer of deceit must be fueling my libido. Had to be, my response to her was off the charts.

"I'm your consolation prize." Mentally, I snickered. She'd wanted the strip mall, then she'd wanted to confront me, but she was going to strip naked for me instead.

I dipped my head and licked the rim of her ear, delighting

in her shiver. Good. I'd make sure I had the upper hand, that I didn't lose my head as soon as she fisted my cock.

Tipping her face back, her lips curled in a lazy smile. "Now show me what I've won."

We stood in the middle of her living room, with only a lamp in the corner on. I checked to make sure the front drapes were drawn. Not because I cared if anyone saw my bare ass pounding into her. Anyone seeing her body on display made me want to envelop her in a cape and fly her away.

I wrapped my hands around her waist to draw her closer, *needing* her closer.

A faint buzzing sound caught my attention. I frowned. Was that a phone?

She groaned and pressed into me. "I'm going to ignore it. If it's important, they'll call back."

Capturing her lush mouth, I proved to her I was grateful for her decision. The wine still flavored her lips, along with her unique, intoxicating taste and the promise of amazing sex. I bunched the hem of her skirt up. Maybe I'd take her fast and hard, relieve the pressure, then spend some time playing with her body.

Her eager response only encouraged my plan.

The vibrating continued. With a frustrated huff, she pulled away.

"Sorry." Her cheeks were flushed and her nipples strained against her shirt. Better than any centerfold I'd ever seen.

While she located her purse and dug around inside, I willed myself not to shove my hand into my pants. My shaft pressed against my waistband and I wanted so badly to find release inside Mara.

She answered the phone and turned her back on me. "What? Yes, yes. Do that and I'll meet her there."

She hung up and stood unmoving, her head hanging and

her shoulders drooping. Genuine disappointment curled in my belly. She'd gotten bad news and the fun was over. When she spun toward me, she wore a false smile.

"I...have to cut the night short." She shrugged, sadness and worry etched in her features.

I refused to acknowledge the tiny bit of worry for her creeping in.

"I'm sorry, Sam."

My dad's name slapped me in the face and reminded me why I was in her place. "Is everything all right? Your store?"

She shook her head. "It's not the store worrying me tonight. Family emergency." Pushing her bangs off her face, she looked around, then down at herself. "I've gotta change clothes. Oh, you need a ride back to the club."

I could offer to call an Uber, aka my driver, but I was reluctant to part ways so soon. I wasn't done with her, on many levels. "Only if it's on the way. Where are you going?"

"Twin City Medical."

My brows shot up. A hospital. Normally, I didn't care about his hookups' personal lives, but Mara was different. I needed to know my target. Learn her weak areas. That was it. Not because I was curious about anything to do with her.

"Go change."

With a grateful smile, she rushed to the back of the house. I buttoned up my shirt and grabbed her keys. Her phone lay where she'd left it and the lock screen wasn't yet showing. Snatching it up and punching in my number, I called myself, then entered my contact info.

Almost too late, I realized I'd typed *Wes*.

"Sam. Fucking Sam," I muttered as I corrected it and added Smith for a generic last name in case she tried looking me up.

"Did you say something?" Mara trotted back down the hall

My hand fell limp at my side, barely clasping her phone. She wore soft jeans that molded to all of her curves and a red "Bazinga" T-shirt. Her gaze fell on her phone in my hand and her brow furrowed.

"I've got my contact info in here for when you want to claim your consolation prize." I jingled her keys. "I'll drive you to the hospital and call a ride from there."

A myriad of emotions ran across her face. Disbelief, regret, relief. "Of course, I want what's mine."

She just missed the mark for playful flirtation and her body language spoke of urgency. I cocked my head in the direction of the car and she charged out the door.

We were back on the road. I was hard and throbbing, but as Mara's tension filled the air, my sex drive waned.

"So what's going on?" I glanced over at her staring out the window, fiddling her thumbs in a solo game of thumb war.

She turned her worried gaze on me. "My mom. She has some medical problems and spiked a high fever. My guess is pneumonia again."

Again? I'd had pneumonia maybe once in my life. What did people say to news like that? My mom would cackle and list the reasons the recipient was deserving of their misfortune.

"Hope she's okay."

"Thanks. She usually gets better, but I always worry if this'll be the time…" Her attention focused back out the passenger window.

Was her mom the reason she'd marked my dad and targeted his money? Didn't make it right, but— *No*. No softening.

I let her drift off. Specific knowledge was what I was after and I wanted to get it myself. She'd already proven she could worm into someone's life enough that they'd dedicate a portion of their fortune to her. No way would I trust another person getting close to her, if I could even get past telling a private investigator my personal business.

I'd do this myself. Sam had as good as abandoned me after the divorce, but I couldn't help but feel protective toward my father. Whatever I had done to drive Sam away, I could make up for it by figuring out why Mara would play with an old man's emotions.

∽

Mara

I WAVED at Sam as he drove off.

He'd showed me where he was going to park my car and he would lock my key inside. I had my fob. I'd offered to stay with him until his Uber arrived, but he'd told me to get to my mom.

My responsible side asked why I had trusted him with my keys. If he stole my car, I could grunt out the deductible and use insurance to buy more reliable wheels. If Sam took it on a joyride and crashed it, well, that'd fit my night perfectly. I sighed and trudged down the corridor toward the emergency room. The nurse from the living center had reported that Mom's breathing was growing more labored. From experience, we both knew nothing short of a hospital stay would help.

Smiling at the girl manning the ER desk, I introduced myself and was shown back to Mom's room.

The quiet bustle of the emergency room always surprised me. TV shows made it look so chaotic, so...urgent. But nurses worked quietly at the counter that circled the middle of the ward, doctors studied charts at pods with screens and keyboards, and any employees and patients in the halls went straight for their destination with little commotion. Once in a while, I'd hear a moan from a patient's room, but even that was rare.

Stillness and warmth encompassed me as I entered the room. The square, white, all-too-familiar space was like any other, except for the suites where patients were curtained off. I dreaded when Mom was put into one of those. Made it all seem more serious.

In the time it'd taken me to get here, the ambulance had already delivered their patient and left. Mom lay resting. I doubted she was asleep with a nasal cannula in and a blood pressure cuff strapped around her arm. An IV ran to her other arm.

I pulled a chair closer and sat.

"Hey," Mom breathed. "Sorry to disrupt your night."

I gave her a reassuring smile. "Oh, you know my Friday nights are never exciting."

I didn't allow my thoughts to settle on Sam and his sparkling blue eyes and broad shoulders. Mom would sense my disappointment and she had more things to worry about, like getting better.

A knock on the door interrupted us a moment before a guy, not much younger than me, entered. He had a ready smile and wore gun-metal gray scrubs.

"I'm here to take Wendy Baranski for an X-ray."

I knew the routine. "That's her. Do you need me with?"

"No. Hold the room down for us and we'll be right back."

I sat back while they rolled the entire cot to X-ray. The quiet hadn't unnerved me when it had been just the two of us in the room, but alone, I couldn't stand it. I numbly surfed through the crappy cable offered by the hospital and waited.

The rest of the night went by with the familiar blur of doctors' reports of pneumonia, treatment plans, admitting her for a hospital stay, and settling her in.

I checked the time, deciding whether I should catch a few hours of sleep in an ungodly uncomfortable chair or head home for a few hours before work.

"Oh my gosh, Mara." Mom's eyes barely stayed open. She was going to sleep soon herself. "Go home and get some rest. I know how busy Saturdays are for you."

"I can always call Chris to man the store." If he was around. My only full-time employee had a life, too. Maybe. Likely a movie to see, at least.

"I'm just going to sleep all night and day. You know how this goes."

Yeah. I did. When Mom had been sick last week, I'd worried that it would result in this. "I'll stop by after work, okay?"

Mom nodded, already drifting off. I leaned down and kissed her cheek, the burn of tears igniting behind my eyes. I neared the doorway and stopped to brush off my cheeks before entering the wide hallway, where nurses darted back and forth.

God, this sucked. Nights like this reinforced my decision to put Mom in a nursing home, but it didn't assuage the guilt any. Even though Mom had urged me to do it, claiming she didn't want her daughter's life to be burdened with caring for a parent's basic needs.

More tears rose. I often thought I should've soldiered on, but I'd seen how hard succumbing to severe multiple sclerosis was for her. Twenty-four-hour care was required and I couldn't provide it. At least I'd secured the money to pay the bills for it.

CHAPTER 3

es

I TAPPED another golf ball across the green. The white, dimpled ball swirled around the hole and dropped in without hesitation.

"*Sick.*" My friend Flynn thumped his club against the ground. "I think you come out and play instead of working all day."

Rapping my club against Flynn's, I strode past him to let my friend have his turn.

For me, there was no play in the workday. A man didn't keep his millions by jacking around instead of making money.

Flynn was the same, it was why he teased me constantly. Equally focused on his own business, he respected my time and space but also kept me from getting lost in my own head.

I dropped my club in the golf bag. Saturday rounds of golf with Flynn comprised much of my rare time away from work. Might as well get in a full day of play before the course closed for the season. The gray sky promised dropping temperatures as the afternoon grew later.

Flynn put his ball and overshot. He swore and glared at the offending green. "I'll beat you at this yet." He settled in for another shot. "Have you notified Sam's piece of ass her reckoning has come?"

"She's been trying to confront me every day since." I gulped as he thought of pink bangs and a little tongue I was sure would've been all over my dick within minutes if it weren't for the phone call.

Laughing, Flynn adjusted his stance to putt again. "What are you waiting for, dude? Rip into her."

Oh, I'd rip into her all right. "Just so happens, I met her at my club."

Flynn's gaze popped off the ball. "And did it get ugly?"

My grin had to look like I'd nailed a hole in one. "No, because I told her my name was Sam."

"Story. Now." Flynn straightened and waited.

Other golfers were making their way to their hole. I didn't care to share my private business with the world. "Make your damn shot and I'll keep talking."

Flynn swung the club down and hit the ball without looking. He cocked a brow toward Wes, not caring where it landed.

"Fine. She came in asking for me, so I went to check her out. I realized who she was and that she didn't know it was me." I lifted a shoulder. "So I decided to tell her my name was Sam and find out what had made my dad willing to hand over a major piece of property to her."

"Did you?"

Yes. "Almost. Supposedly, she got a call that her mom was in the hospital."

"You don't believe her?"

"Maybe. It'd be a good setup." I had thought about it while waiting for my driver. She'd mysteriously gotten a call and called it quits before we'd hit it. It wasn't like a hookup would follow her into the ER, but she could snag my sympathy and use it to squeeze me dry.

"So now what?"

I pinned my friend with a determined stare. "Now I wait for her to call. I can sample the goods while getting my revenge."

I'd expected a fist bump from Flynn, but he wore a slight frown. "What if she plays you, too?"

"No way. I'm in this with my eyes open. She's the one who doesn't know who I am."

"Whatever, dude. Keep me posted so I can tell you to abort the mission when she starts draining your wallet. She's going out of business thanks to you, by the way."

I studied Flynn. Genuine concern emanated from him. As if Mara could get one over on me.

We hopped into the golf cart and jetted to the next hole.

"So, what's she look like?" Flynn draped his arm over the wheel and flashed the dimple-baring grin that brought the girls flocking, along with the limit-free credit card.

I blew out a breath. I wished I could say she looked like a wet mutt that'd been homeless and out in the rain for a month. "Pretty, in a simple way. Beautiful, really, and all without much makeup." I settled back and let the images of Mara laughing and dancing run through my head. "She had her hair in ponytails, but it was cute. She's short, too, but doesn't seem like it because she's not, like, meek or anything."

Flynn studied me, saying nothing.

Irritation spiked. "What?"

"I thought you'd just say she's hot. Or she's fugly. But I'd swear you're going to break out in song, spout some poetry."

I clenched my jaw. I wasn't enamored.

I wasn't.

"I have to know my target."

Flynn grunted but didn't sound convinced.

"I know it might all be contrived. Mara's a woman in a male-dominated business. I doubt Sam was the only one who 'helped' her along the way."

Especially after seeing her house. Had all of her money gone into the store, or had she spent it on exotic vacations? I made a note to check into it.

A simple, bordering on rundown, house would give the effect that she had nothing and needed help.

We climbed out of the cart and chose our next clubs. Flynn asked, "When do you see her again?"

"After this, I'll go to the office and get some work done. If she hasn't called by then, I'll text her."

"Maybe you should play hard to get."

What if that kept me from her bed? No, I wanted more than a nibble of Mara Jade.

~

Mara

I RUBBED my eyes and blinked away my tiredness. It didn't help.

"Are you all right?" Ephraim, one of my regulars, glanced at me while he meticulously arranged the pieces of his Axis & Allies game. The light from my store danced over his dark scalp as he bent over the table. He was probably about my mom's age, but where my mom was dependent on a wheelchair, he was trim and fit with an athletic six-foot frame.

I shot him a reassuring smile. "Late night for all the wrong reasons."

"Your mom?"

My heart twisted. Not just at the reminder of why I'd been up late, but that my regulars had become such a mainstay of my life, not just my store. I considered many of them friends. They gave me sound business advice and recommended various items I should stock. I rarely failed to heed their advice—after much consideration, of course, thanks to therapy.

"She's in the hospital again. I can't thank you enough for recommending Golden Meadows Living Center. They've taken such good care of her." I thanked my lucky stars that I could afford quality care for my mom every time I walked into the clean, cheery facility.

Ephraim's expression crinkled with tenderness. He inspected the minute game pieces before setting each one down. "They took good care of my dad, and then Mom when she developed dementia. I'm glad it's working out." He straightened and clapped his hands. "So where are these players you promised me?"

The door chimed and another frequent customer entered.

Mara grinned. "Here's at least one. Over here, Joe."

Magic players, none of them old enough to drink, were already deep into their game at the tables in the corner. More teenagers lined the monitors, comatose at the Xbox while trying various video games. Another piece of advice from my clientele. I sold many games because they were able to try them out first at my store. Or it drew them into my store, where they spent money on other items.

Joe grinned as he approached, his features always what I'd thought of as fatherly. Probably because he had five grown kids. "Where's this hours-long strategy game you mentioned?"

She introduced the two men. "I think Stella said she'd be a

little late, but you two go ahead and set it up since it takes forever."

Ephraim paused over his setup. "Have you heard from the big guy's kid yet?"

My shoulders stiffened. I hadn't told my customers about the store closing. Five weeks remained before I had to shut my doors. Monday I'd put up the notice. I'd give myself today to pretend it was business as usual.

Another day where Sam wouldn't be strolling in with his booming laugh and Star-Trek-versus-Star-Wars mentality. He would've hated a game like Axis & Allies, but he'd wander the store and chat up the young players, coax their future dreams out of them and encourage their ability. More than once, I'd caught the wistful, and often remorseful, look on his face when he thought no one was looking.

Poor guy. Money hadn't saved him from heartbreak. Probably caused it.

I rested back on a table. Usually, on Saturdays, I made rounds to everyone playing, manned the register, and did menial cleaning. It was early yet, so not many paying customers roamed the place.

"Do you know anything about him?" I asked.

If anyone knew, it'd be Ephraim. On weekdays, he'd come in for the monthly pile of comics I reserved for him and he'd be dressed in a sharp suit and tie. I'd discovered he was a lawyer and we often discussed the business goings-on in the city. He was a wealth of information. Today he was slightly dressed down in pressed slacks and a polo.

He drummed his fingers on the back of a chair. "I heard that Wesley Robson thinks himself the next real estate tycoon. He put a bid on a stretch across the river, thinks St. Paul needs a premium outlet mall."

One never *needed* an outlet mall, but I enjoyed the one in Albertville. No one would guess by my daily choice in clothing: jeans or leggings, simple tops, and shoes that dated back to my college days. Going into fall, I might throw on a flannel to set off whatever color I had in my hair.

But my shopping days were limited, at least until I found another job or reopened my store somewhere else. Did I dare use any of my stored funds to do that?

"Sam talked about him and what he did for a living, but they weren't close when he died." We'd gotten into long, in-depth discussions about their various family issues, but Sam's family drama made mine minuscule in comparison.

Joe quietly read through directions for the game, but his furtive glances hinted he was eavesdropping.

Ephraim took a seat and frowned at the board. "I've heard bits here and there. He's been buying up property in more than Minnesota. There was a kerfuffle in New York because he purchased a place that locals wanted to restore." His brows pinched. I guessed the young Robson hadn't restored the place.

"Mr. Robson isn't a people person." Joe abandoned the instructions and picked up figures from the game to inspect them one by one.

"You know him?" A surge of excitement falsely lifted my spirits. Even if Joe was besties with Wesley Robson, I didn't have a leg to stand on. He owned the strip mall and he wanted to demolish it.

Joe pushed up his wire-rimmed glasses and pointed across the street where an office building loomed over her store. Also Wes's property, his main offices I'd learned when I'd gone hunting him for answers. "I work for him. Maintenance."

He'd mentioned what he did for a living before, but he didn't often discuss work. But perhaps he'd be willing to fill me in. Although his somber tone didn't encourage me that

I'd get anywhere when I was finally able to track Wesley Robson down. "That bad?"

Joe fiddled with the figures. "He's in it for the money."

I realized we were talking about the man's ultimate boss. No reason to threaten Joe's employment, too. I changed the subject. "I didn't know you worked so close by."

He bobbed his head and we fell into easy chatting that transitioned into gaming. I forgot my troubles as the store grew busier. If I'd been able to stay, I would've had to think about hiring someone for the weekends and even being open for a few hours on Sunday.

But no more. My excitement and optimism that my store would grow and be successful for decades, sustaining me and my employees, were dashed.

I had to find that man and talk to him.

CHAPTER 4

ara

MY STOMACH RUMBLED as I sat bedside with Mom. I should've grabbed supper, but work had been busy and I hadn't wanted to put off the hospital visit. By working all day, I'd missed all the doctors' rounds and updates.

Mom glanced away from the latest superhero movie I had brought. "Even I heard that. Go eat."

"I can stay a little longer." I palmed my phone and lied to myself that I wasn't waiting for Sam to call. But who was I kidding? He was sweet enough to drive me to the hospital, but I doubted I'd made enough of an impression to warrant him hunting me down.

Unless he had other plans with someone else. No, I wouldn't go down that road, being suspicious of every prospective guy.

"Mara." Mom sighed. "I love having you around but not

when it costs you your own health. I'm going to fall asleep soon. Go grab a bite and get some rest."

The corner of my mouth lifted. Always a mother. "Okay, but I want to be here tomorrow to hear what the doctors have to say."

"They'll probably release me. I'm feeling better and not in the middle of a flare-up." She shifted in the bed as much as she could. Her disease had robbed much of her mobility. Some people lived decades with MS, but Mom had deteriorated rapidly.

My phone vibrated. A ping of excitement speared me. Could it be?

Maybe it was just Chris telling me about a new find on eBay we should purchase for the store. I dabbled in pawning collectibles, but only because he had oodles of knowledge and a passion for it. It'd made a nice income stream on top of my regular sales. Chris got a raise and permission to fully geek out over an old tin Spiderman lunch box, and the store garnered a solid reputation.

I peeked at my screen.

Holy moly! It read *Sam*. Hungry?

I jerked my gaze back up to my mom, who watched me with interest.

"Hot date?" Mom's lips quirked.

"Maybe." I relished these moments where we could be a normal mom and daughter.

"Good. Don't let him break your heart."

I kissed Mom goodbye and rushed out of the hospital room. I texted back.

I haven't eaten yet. Meet at Blue Hound?

An immediate answer. Can I get dropped off there?

A thousand yeses! U like driving my car that much?

Gimme ur keys.

With a grin, I strained to keep from sprinting out of the hospital.

~

Wes

I DUBIOUSLY EYED the burger joint. This was where Mara wanted to eat?

She'd invited me and I'd half expected her to choose a place with a price tag that she'd *let* me pick up. After a day of golfing, I wasn't overdressed for Blue Hound. Hell, I didn't think there was a way to underdress.

Instead of sleek lines, the exterior was comprised of roughened wood and cheap paneling. Whenever the door opened, rowdy laughter drifted out. The smell of meat-on-grill teased my stomach, but I doubted the cut of meat was close to any quality my personal chef used.

A car engine turned my head. Mara and her reliable sedan were pulling in. I tracked her progress like a guard dog, ignoring the thrill at her arrival.

She killed the engine and got out, but I still couldn't see her. Darkness set in Minnesota well before nine p.m. this time of year. Light glowing from street lamps scattered around the parking lot highlighted the messy style she'd thrown her hair up in. When she cleared the cars, she looked just as adorable and doable as when she'd changed out of her clubbing clothes. Black and red leggings—was that an Iron Man design?—and an oversized red sweater with a lightning bolt.

Mixing Marvel and DC. Equal opportunity fangirl?

And the fact that I knew the difference… I mentally shook my head.

I frowned. She'd said she hadn't eaten yet, but I hadn't thought about why. Arcadia closed at six on Saturdays. I knew, I'd done my research on the place.

What had she been doing?

She faltered when she noticed my expression.

I smiled, purposely infusing warmth into my expression. "There she is."

"I didn't think you'd beat me here." She crossed her arms to ward off the chill in the air.

I wouldn't be surprised if she had a Wookie coat stashed away.

"Traffic was light." I'd been in the area. My office was close by. So was Arcadia. Must be how she knew about this place. I opened the door for her.

Stepping in, I cringed when my running shoes crunched on peanut shells. Good thing I hadn't changed clothes before I'd spent the evening working. Crunching my Paul Andrews through shells and burger grease would get my account at Barneys New York suspended.

The dull roar in the restaurant wasn't unlike my club, but it was more boisterous. Odd, since there wasn't a dance floor. Booths and tables and peanut shells as far as I could see.

Mara slid her hand into mine and pulled me toward the bar. "They have the best food here. I thought about stopping at the hospital cafeteria, but I got out of work late and by the time I got there, they'd shut down the grill. I wanted real food."

I dropped her hand like it was hot when I realized I didn't want to let go of it to sit. We settled at a table and a young woman took our order. I didn't fail to notice the special smile she gave me. As long as the girl didn't know who I really was, I wouldn't give her a second thought.

I caught Mara's smirk.

"That must happen to you everywhere." No jealousy tinged her words.

She was right. It did. I rolled a shoulder and sipped my water. "It must to you, too."

She barked out a laugh and then paused when she saw I wasn't chuckling. "Oh, you're serious. Not really, no."

Either she was playing coy or she was truly oblivious. When my bartender had called, he'd labeled her a "hot chick." The young host of this joint had damn near wet himself to greet her when they'd walked in. Her girl-next-door appeal must be what caught the men. And those damn leggings showing off her curves.

I decided it was time to dig for info. "How's your mom?"

She pursed her lips and stirred her soda. "She's better than last night. Meds are working."

I waited. She didn't offer more. As far as cons go, it wasn't an elaborate one. How often had her mom been "in the hospital" when she'd been with Sam? "That's good then. Must be a relief."

She nodded and I thought back to when Sam had been in the hospital after his first heart attack. I hadn't found out until after my dad's double bypass when his assistant had called to request me to take over some of the daily affairs that Sam couldn't attend to. *Didn't want to worry you, kid*, Sam had roughly growled over the phone.

Sam hadn't been concerned about what worried me since I was fourteen.

"So, what do you do again?" She brushed her hair out of her eyes.

Why'd I think it was cuter than hell when she did that?

I picked a career that wasn't really a lie but that would call to her greedy instincts. "I'm in sales."

She brightened. "Really? Like what?"

My grin turned a little smug. Knew she'd take the bait. "Mergers and acquisitions, mostly. Nothing exciting, really. I just finished the purchase of some property in New York."

Disgust flickered through her features.

Not the reaction I'd been expecting. "That bad?"

"Oh no. Sorry." She gave me a sheepish grin. "At work today, one of my customers told me about how the guy who's putting me out of business just purchased a possible landmark and remodeled it, destroying any historical value it might've had."

I ground my teeth. Landmark my ass. That old hotel had been trash. There'd been so much human and rat waste inside, my crews had worn hazard suits when gutting it. I'd ask if she had read any real data on the deal or the building, but then she might actually look it up and see my picture.

"The guy sounds better and better." I couldn't help the hard note in my voice, but from her agreement, she interpreted it as outrage about *the guy who's putting her out of business.*

"Right? I can't believe he'd be so different from his dad."

I fought the angry set of my mouth into a neutral position. I wasn't supposed to know anything about this. I wanted to ask how I was so much different than Sam. It wasn't like people handed realty over to the man. Sam had played just as dirty in business as he had in Wes's personal life.

There, we'd been alike. As far as looks went, we couldn't have been more opposite. Sam had been shorter than me by two inches, with dusty blond hair before it'd gone gray. He'd had a stocky build, not the lean frame I assumed came from my mom.

"You knew his dad?"

Sadness lit her eyes. "He was the Sam I mentioned that

passed away." She chuckled. "When I leased the property, I'd never met him, but I got a kick out of his assistant."

Yeah, Franklin was a *kick* all right. If you called disapproving glances every time I handed him an order a good time.

"Then I went to TC Comic-Con and I wore my usual Mara Jade costume—my mom named me after Luke Skywalker's wife—and this robust man dressed as," her laugh tinkled around me like crystals, "not a Starfleet captain, but an *admiral*. Can you believe it? I thought, here's a guy who thinks outside of the box. Anyway, he asked me about my costume. When I told him I was named after the Star Wars character, he realized I was the one who'd just leased his storefront and we chatted all night."

Delight ran across her face and I could only stare. My heart slammed into my feet. Rage churned and threatened to reject the water I sipped.

My dad had used to take me to that comic book convention. Another one of the traditions that'd been lost in the divorce. Had Sam attended to pick up women half his age?

She unfolded her napkin and refolded it, her eyes glittering with unshed tears. "He started coming into my store after that and we would get to talking." She looked up at the ceiling like she was fighting the spill of tears. "He was such a mentor."

I was about to snidely inquire how an old man mentored a pretty young lady, but the spell was broken when the server delivered our meals.

Mara let out a groan that went straight to my cock. "I'm starving. This looks delicious."

My manhood completely forgot the girl had been gushing about my father. All it cared about were the memories of how good she'd promised to be in bed. Or in the car.

We ate and chatted. I'd been planning to wait until she was finished before asking her more about the store, but my phone vibrated.

I pulled it out and saw it was Franklin. What the hell? If there were problems at my club, it'd be my own assistant, Helen, calling. Franklin only handled Robson Industries, what I'd inherited from Sam.

"I have to take this." I slid out of the booth and aimed for the front of the restaurant, where the din was lower. "What's going on?"

"Sorry to disturb you, Mr. Robson." Franklin treated me the same as Sam, except I heard the undercurrents of a scowl. "I'm afraid there's a protest on the property in NYC. Some of the construction equipment has been vandalized."

"Are we talking spray paint or damage?"

"Both, sir. Police are reporting they're still there, camping out on the property."

"Arrest them all. Trespassing and defacing private property."

Franklin hesitated. "Yes, Mr. Robson."

There it was. The censure Franklin never failed to give.

"What, Franklin?" I bit the words out. Why did I keep the guy on, and in such a high position? Yes, I could trust him. Franklin knew his way around the business and every facet of Sam's old empire.

It couldn't be sentimentality.

"While you'd be within your rights, I don't think such an abrupt action will sit well with the citizens of NYC that care about the history of the building."

"Its history was full of piss and vomit and empty needles. Even the rats decided to find a better place to live."

"None of them are arguing that it could've been condemned. They fear that it's a sign of the future. You come in and build, possibly buy more property, or someone else will. They can barely afford to live in the neighborhood now. If that happens, they fear not just losing the meaning behind their home, but being the homeless ones roaming from abandoned building to abandoned building."

Well, the New Yorkers were right about one thing. I was throwing around an amount for an offer to the neighboring structure's owner. Everyone could be bought, and I had a banker friend who was interested in expanding into New York. If word of this silliness got around, my friend might back out and find another space, as well as think I was weak and lacked backbone. I couldn't let the Robson name down.

"Tell the police to arrest them all. Give them whatever information they need to press charges." I ended the call.

I glared out of the picture window by the entrance, clenching and unclenching a fist. That NYC purchase had plagued me with nothing but problems. The one-point-eight-million dollar condo I was in the middle of buying in Manhattan would be worthless if I had to endure the constant headache of protesters every time I sealed a deal. Why the hell did I want to live in New York again?

Winters that didn't reach twenty below zero, for one.

No, I'd act hard and swift. Then I'd be the one to buy the whole block and really give them something to complain about.

"Everything all right?"

I almost jumped at Mara's question. I turned and looked past her to the booth where we'd been sitting. A young man was bussing our table.

She saw where I looked and waved it off. "I got the bill. I hope you don't mind not hanging out here long. Home sounds nice after a long day."

I got the bill. Had any of my dates ever picked up the tab?

My mother never bought me dinner, but Mara didn't know for sure my pockets were lined and loaded.

"Thanks. How can I ever pay you back?" My crooked smile infused heat into her gaze. So easy.

She jingled the keys. "Think you can find the way to my place again?"

CHAPTER 5

ara

I COULDN'T UNLOCK my door fast enough and I didn't bother turning on the light. No need. The flames that had ignited between us the previous night burned hotter than ever. The mysterious phone call had threatened to put a hitch in my night, but I shoved it out of my mind. I wasn't young and naïve anymore, but I wasn't going to suspect every guy I dated of deceiving me.

I wanted him, wanted his touch all over my body. If anyone could wipe out the stress over my business closing, the shitty news of my mom sick in the hospital, and the dismal outlook of my life in general, it'd be the man who'd just rested his hands on my hips.

Tonight, more than last night, I needed an escape from Mara Jade Baranski's life. Sam might be a fleeting fling, but he was what the doctor had ordered.

Don't get tangled up with a man just because he's good looking.

Make sure he's more handsome inside than out. My mother's cautionary advice should be heeded, but I didn't have it in me tonight. Mom hadn't expected my dad to leave without a care. I didn't expect Sam to stay. There was a difference. If more grew out of my physical relationship with Sam—win. If he walked, well, the complication of a man had no place in my life now anyway.

Sam's caress moved up my rib cage until his hands draped my shoulders. He squeezed. I moaned. A massage would rival sex.

"I have a debt to settle with you." His breath whispered over me. He kissed my neck. "Are you cold?"

His teasing tone implied he knew he'd caused my reaction. He straightened and kneaded my shoulders. I dropped my purse and rolled my head back and forth.

So much tension.

He reached around my front, lifted my sweater, and slipped it off, dropping more kisses on my neck. I moaned and pressed into him. Next, he removed my cami.

The small circles he rubbed up and down my back were divine. How had my knees not buckled?

My bra was unhooked and my breath froze. Fast and furious was the pace I'd anticipated after last night, not slow and sensual.

Warm hands cupped my breasts and he rolled my nipples between his fingers. I leaned back against his chest until he was the only reason I remained standing. Threading my hands through his hair, I enjoyed the multitude of sensations. A gorgeous man at my back, his strong hands stroking me, his soft hair tickling my fingers.

In a sudden movement, he swooped me up. I gasped and grabbed for him.

His hot look of pure desire robbed me of words. Did my expression mirror his?

He must've remembered where my room was from when I'd changed, not that there were many places to go in my small house. Without pause, he stretched me out on the bed. So glad I'd made it this morning and it wasn't in its normal state of disarray.

With a searing look of promise, he rolled me over and continued his sensual massage.

So. Good.

I whined in complaint when he stopped.

He chuckled. "Don't worry, I'm not done." An easy tug on my hips and I rolled onto my back.

His gaze snagged on my chest. my swollen breasts were slightly reddened from his touch, my nipples jutting toward the ceiling. Peeling down my leggings, he raised his hot gaze to mine.

"Did you know mixing your comic brands is a felony?"

A guy who could tell the difference—*hot*. "You'll have to punish me."

He released one foot from my leggings, then the other, not breaking eye contact. I clung to his words, terrified we'd get interrupted again, that life would intervene like it always did.

"You won't believe how much I need this." My words spilled out, a plea for him not to stop.

He cocked a brow and a smug grin lifted his lips. Dancing his fingers over my bare legs, he worked his way up to my panties and laid his hand on my sex. "Oh, I think I can tell."

I panted and rocked my hips, my legs spreading of their own accord. He shifted so his palm pressed against my clit.

With a growl, he flipped me again.

"You're driving me crazy." I bowed into the hand he'd laid at the small of my back.

"I said I wasn't done with the massage yet."

He kneaded the muscles of my back and I transformed

into putty. His weight depressed the bed next to me, his masculine presence overwhelming the room. None of my previous boyfriends had had that effect. They hadn't had Sam's broad shoulders or anything close to the suggestion of biceps bulging through his shirt.

I would get to see him naked tonight. My stomach fluttered. Not normally self-conscious, I hoped I wouldn't be when an Adonis like him stripped down. Because I was wearing just panties, and putting more clothes on now wasn't an option. Not until I orgasmed hard. A few times.

He bent toward me, close to my head. "Are you relaxed yet?"

His baritone rumbled through me. Relaxed as in muscles not tense? Yes. Sexually relaxed? Stupid question.

His weight lifted and clothing rustled. No way was I missing a second of his bare skin.

The cozy sweater he'd been wearing was off and he was drawing his T-shirt over his head. With my exhale, my body sank farther into the bed. What. A. Sight.

Inch after inch of bronzed skin dipped and curved over solid muscle. I'd only seen abs like that on magazine covers. Defined pecs flexed and lifted as he unsnapped his pants.

Ooh, and the biceps. I was an arm girl and I rarely got to feel up guns. Shoving his hand in a pocket, he withdrew a condom and tossed it on the bed before going back to undressing.

I sucked in air. His pants were coming off. God, they looked expensive. I didn't know anything about brand names, but I'd guess his pair hadn't been purchased in a second-hand store or even an outlet store.

He must do well in sales. How did a guy with a white-collar job maintain a body like that?

"See something you like?"

My smile was coy. I never smiled like that! I rolled to my

side and used an arm as a kickstand for my head so I could keep my gaze on him. "I don't know. I mean, you should start going to the gym once in a while."

He paused, toeing off his shoes to get his pants off, then a low chuckle sounded before he straightened. "I'll think about it."

Only his black, sporty boxer-briefs stood in the way and they were doing a piss-poor job. The swollen head of his cock pushed past the waistband.

A swell of female pride puffed my chest. I had done that to him and I hadn't even touched him yet.

I hadn't touched him yet.

Rising to my knees, I crawled to the edge of the bed. His gaze took on a predatory glint. I rimmed the top of his underwear with my fingers. The words printed on the band weren't a style I'd heard of, and his underclothes looked like nothing I'd find where I shopped.

Unwrapping my present to myself, I freed him. Long, thick, and proud, he remained still and let me skim my hand up and down his shaft. It pulsed and the heat radiating off his skin stoked my excitement.

It was playtime, and I had one question. "Do I need to delve into my flavored-condom stash?"

Wes

MY GAZE WAS RIVETED on Mara's lips. "I'm clean," I managed to choke out. I played it safe most of the time, but I regularly saw a private physician. "Do whatever you want." *As long as it means sucking my dick.*

Was she going to? The expression on her face said it all and it affected me more than any other woman I'd been with.

Why? I suspected she was a user, but with her full breasts lifting with each breath she took, it became less of an issue. The memory of her supple body under my fingertips threw me off my game.

I needed to take charge again, to remember that I controlled this situation. I meant to push her back, but her mouth closed around the tip of my cock as her hand wrapped around it. My hips bucked and my grip landed on her head.

A flick of her tongue and my head fell back with a groan. I fisted both hands in her hair, loosening her hair clip. Damn thing was in the way. I plucked the clasp out. Thick waves of pink-tinted, downy brown hair spilled over her shoulders.

She created an erotic sight. Her mouth wrapped around my cock, her eyes closed, her fist pumping the base. Those beautiful hazel eyes of hers flicked open to meet my gaze. They lit with mirth and she dragged her teeth along my sensitized flesh.

"Oh god." I concentrated on not shoving her head closer, testing if she could relax her throat.

Yesss. She could. The woman had a mouth and I was going to spend my load in less than sixty seconds.

"Enough." Cupping her chin, I drew her off me.

She licked her lips and scooted back on the bed. Maybe I should prep her, but by her glistening sex, she was ready. With Mara reclining before me, I retrieved the condom, ripped it open, and rolled it on. I hated the squeeze of the plastic, wished it wasn't necessary, but it'd allow me to be inside Mara and that was all I cared about.

Dimly, the design of her duvet cover registered.

We were going to fuck on the Bat-Signal. It'd be a first for me, and I kind of wanted to pump my fist in the air.

I kneeled on the bed and slid her panties off. Then, I laid a hand on each of her knees and shoved them apart.

She audibly sucked in a breath while mine *whooshed* out. Fine, dusky hair framed her swollen pink labia, slightly separated to reveal her arousal tucked in between. I'd tasted her twenty-four hours ago and still felt like a starving man.

She squirmed and her movements only opened her more. My cock throbbed, demanded release, but I wanted her to feel just as crazy.

Using one finger, I swirled it around her entrance. She fell back on her elbows, watching me. Once I was covered in her juices, I circled her clit and was rewarded with a moan. The firm bud pulsed against my pad. I wanted to suck on it, but the drive to thrust into her hard enough to make her breasts bounce was stronger.

But first, I trailed my fingertip down until I entered her. Her hips rose in encouragement. Withdraw, enter, I pumped my digit a few more times until she took a shuddering breath.

I switched out my hand for my cock. Forward momentum met some resistance—I must be larger than she was used to. Not an uncommon occurrence for me. Inch by inch, I fed my length inside, my gaze glued to where she encircled my erection. She suddenly clutched my shoulders while she wiggled to adjust.

Finally seated fully inside of her wet heat, I dragged my gaze up her flushed body to her face. A hint of trepidation remained in her expression.

"I won't hurt you." Why did I feel like I was lying? I meant physically, but my spirit rebelled, urging me to be true to my word.

I withdrew before I could dwell on the foreign emotion any longer and slammed back into her. She gasped and her fingers dug into my shoulders, but it wasn't pain in her features.

"You're just so...big." A lazy grin spread across her face.

I matched it. "Darling, I never tire of hearing that."

She let out a laugh, but another thrust turned it into a whimper for more. Pull out. Thrust. Repeat.

I curled down to cover one nipple with my mouth. Her arms circled my neck as her hips rocked against mine. Tension built, energy crackling between us; our heavy breathing and the slap of flesh on flesh filled the room. Closer. I needed to be closer to her.

I snaked an arm under one of her knees and as I trailed kisses from her chest to her neck. I lifted her leg up and out to the side.

Yes, that helped. I ground into her.

"Sam!"

Fuck! That name. It wasn't mine and it reminded me why I was in her bedroom.

I reared up to watch myself dominate her body. Did she think she could control a man? *I'll*—I pounded harder—*show*—her walls quivered around my cock—*her*.

"Oh— I can't—" She collapsed back, her arms above her head as I completely took over her body.

She yelled, moaned, twisted the blankets in her grip, and she came. Hard. It was like a death grip on my cock. Only the lubrication of her orgasm prevented me from being at a standstill.

My balls tightened. If the sight of her sucking me off was erotic, her climaxing, completely undone from my strokes, was magnificent. I clenched my teeth, a growl starting deep and rumbling out, my thrusts shortening.

"Mara—" I cut myself off before I could declare *you're mine.*

Throwing my head back, I roared, my shout echoing off the walls and mingling with her cries.

My climax was the strongest in recent memory. In all memory.

It went on and on. Jet after jet of cum spurted from me. My condom was already at max capacity. I jerked out of her before it busted, then collapsed on top of her.

Her hold immediately encompassed me and she peppered my face with light kisses.

I blinked. Did she think I needed comforting?

Oddly enough, it felt like I did because it was soothing. I was reluctant to move. But this was when I was going to jump up and tell her who I was. Otherwise, why had I let her think she'd seduced me?

There was another condom in my wallet. And she'd mentioned also having some. It wouldn't hurt to be Sam a little longer. Besides, my question, why she'd messed with my dad, hadn't been answered.

I opened my eyes, but my lids were heavy. I kissed her in return, lingering longer than I expected to before breaking away. "Get under the covers. I'll be right back."

Her satisfied expression couldn't be missed as she did what I said. Finding her bathroom wasn't hard in a house this small. The entire bathroom could fit inside my shower. A tub, a dripping sink with six inches of counter space on each side, and a toilet. That was it.

The condom landed in the trash and I leaned on the sink. Two seconds of looking in the mirror were all I could take. Mussed hair, flushed cheeks, and a chest that was still heaving from the power of climaxing.

Why was I standing here? I wasn't one to linger. I either hopped into bed for round two or left. After the second, sometimes the third time, I vamoosed. Didn't want to give my dates the wrong impression, and work was always waiting.

It was part of the plan. Crawling back into bed with her. Part of my scheme. If I kept telling myself that, it'd excuse the earth-shattering connection I'd felt when we'd climaxed together.

CHAPTER 6

ara

I SWIVELED MY HIPS, and the man under me bared his teeth like a graphic novel bad guy. He filled me, his length knocking on my cervix—near-instant orgasm. But I held all the cards and used my power to bring him to the brink and back off.

"You're evil," he gritted out between clenched teeth.

My throaty laugh was so unlike me. I was not a prude, but last night through to this morning, I'd been an unrepentant sex goddess.

How many times could a woman come in one night?

A lot, that was how many.

Sam grasped my hips.

I shot him a hard look and stilled. "That's not part of our deal."

A brief tightening and he released her to dig his fingers into the edge of the couch.

I resumed riding him. Dry and sore is how I should feel, but when his cock rose to full glory, my body prepped itself.

Grabbing the top of the couch brought my chest against his face. He wasted no time. The guy was magic with his tongue. After he'd prowled out of the bathroom and gotten between the covers with me, he'd kept going until his head had settled between my legs.

A flood rushed to my core at the memory—Sam moving under my comforter, the twin points of my knees tenting the blankets over his head, the thunderous build of another peak. I pumped myself up and down.

He released my nipple with a pop and spoke with a hoarse voice. "Are you finally going to let me come?"

"Uh-huh," I gasped.

His cock swelled inside me. How could he do that, grow impossibly bigger?

Fingernails dug into the fabric. I'd have fuzzies to dig out later. Totally worth it. From the way his biceps bulged, veins protruding from gripping the cushions, so would he.

He thrust his hips up to meet my downward push. "Fuck me, Mara."

"Don't you dare let go." I didn't, either, otherwise, I'd rake my fingernails down his chest, again.

My score marks turned me on more.

It started. The world closed in until it was just the two of us. The coarse hair on his legs tickled my ass each time I rolled over him.

I cried out, the force of our movements banging the couch against the wall. God, that angle felt good. I did it again. My orgasm slammed into me and I pulsed around Sam as he jerked, yelling out his own stream of obscenities as he came.

My only coherent thought was how I'd love to feel those

hot jets release inside of me, coating my core like a balm to cool the fire we formed together.

I shook and gasped as aftershocks set in. With a sigh, I sank into him.

In the four times we'd had sex I'd learned this was my favorite part. No uncomfortable *so what do we do now?* Just postcoital relaxation.

I smiled even though he couldn't see it. I'd had my way with him. Strung it out as long as possible before I had to face adulting for the day.

His arms wrapped around me, his head buried in my neck.

Teeth scraped my skin and I shivered.

"What are you doing?" He couldn't be ready for more?

"I'm hungry."

My eyes flew open. The last time he'd said that he'd landed between my legs again. Sam had a serious thing for oral sex.

"I can't possibly..." I knew I could. Because Sam would get me off.

The arrogant tilt to his mouth sent tingles to my toes.

"I want you to stay right"—he lifted me off his cock and boosted me up so he could slide down to the floor—"here."

He lowered me to my knees on the cushions, legs spread.

Sam had reclined against the couch and placed his head between my legs, his greedy gaze licking up my body to meet mine.

The sheer naughtiness of the position flamed any lingering desire that hadn't yet dissipated. Would it ever around him? There'd be no choice. He'd leave and I'd have to face reality.

Real-life was waiting for me, but in my string of selfish moves, I wanted this. One more round of Sam carrying me away to a place where the dreaded hospital visits and doctors' reports couldn't reach.

He gripped my thighs and lowered me to his mouth.

This was totally happening! I flinched, my over-sensitized clit shocked at the swipe of his tongue. I bit my lip and forced myself to remain still. Orgasms from Sam were something from a different dimension. I'd have to call them Samgasms.

I hitched a breath in a giggle, but the scrape of his teeth overrode my squirms and put me in *oh yeah* territory.

His blue gaze pierced me, the intensity staggering. My eyes fluttered closed as a moan left me. My hands were back to clutching the back of the couch. I would never view this piece of furniture the same way again. It was promoted to the loveseat of ecstasy.

His hold tightened when I tried to rock my hips.

"What? Is this payback?" I lowered my gaze and found his full of intent. Yes. It was.

One of his hands loosened and skimmed along the curve of my ass. Another moan escaped. I was going to be hoarse before he finished with me.

His other hand clamped me to his face, while his roaming fingers circled my sex. I was still slick from minutes ago when I'd come all over him. He pushed two digits in. I wrenched the back of the couch.

His tongue lapping at me, and the instant fullness propelled me higher. *Ride him*, my brain screamed but his strength outmatched mine.

He pumped his fingers. I wailed, falling against the cushions, warm from when he'd rested against them.

No slow build. He attacked my clit, his tongue flicking, his teeth nipping. He wasn't gentle with his hands. Tremors built and I tensed my sore abs. I excused myself from exercising for a week after a night with Sam.

My toes curled, I clawed at the fabric and bore down. Not even he was strong enough to keep me from rocking in time with his thrusts.

"Oh god, Sam!" When I cried his name during sex, it was like a power boost. He became ruthless.

Harder nips, more vigor. Nothing in the world mattered but his mouth on me, his hand driving me wild.

"Yes!" The couch rocked. "Yes!" My forehead almost hit the wall. "Yes!" A muscle pulled in my shoulder.

I crested the peak and shouted yes over and over again. Nearly choking on my tongue, I shoved at his head to get him to stop. My heart wouldn't survive another round. Neither would my poor, old couch.

Freed, I collapsed to the side, facing the back of the couch and breathing heavily.

I looked over my shoulder when he moved. Smug. His expression was smug.

"I'm going to go clean up." His voice was gruff, almost abrupt.

When he rose, his cock was hard once again, but he headed toward the bathroom.

I was in no condition to take care of his erection, but a thread of hurt wove through me. Maybe he knew better than to reuse a condom. Perhaps he had somewhere he needed to be.

I sighed. The hospital was where *I* needed to be. I checked the time: ten a.m. The doctors either made their rounds early or pushed their visits later and later into the day, leaving me wondering whether my mom would go home or spend another night.

Shoving myself up, I was grateful my store was closed on Sundays. I trudged to my bedroom as I heard the shower kick on. A smile tugged at my lips. A hot guy in my shower. I'd dated good-looking guys, but none had had more than two abs or towered over me and blocked out the sun with the width of their shoulders.

I stopped after flipping on the light in my room. Holy messy bedroom, Batman. Covers draped from the bed to the floor. Clothes scattered everywhere. My nightstand drawer hung open from when we'd dived into my condom stash.

If I could fist-bump myself, I would. A girl needed to cut loose with a guy who did it for her. And Sam did.

My heart sank. And today was probably as far as it would go. Searching my drawers for shorts and a cami, I mulled over what the rest of my day would entail. The hospital. That was it.

The water turned off. I didn't need long. If I lingered under the spray, I'd miss time with Sam and get stuck ruminating over my mom and the store.

Mom and the store. One couldn't seem to exist with the other. The portion of my trust I'd used to open Arcadia was all I had. The rest secured Mom's future and medical bills, like the last two nights. Pilfering more to open in another location wasn't an option.

I blinked furiously. Sam couldn't catch me being the girl who cried after sex. How mortifying.

The bathroom door opened. He stepped out and my insides danced. With his black hair slicked back, his blue eyes were more apparent. Water droplets rolled down his chest to the chartreuse towel slung low on his hips.

He glanced at the towel and shrugged. "Your Superman towel was too small."

He passed me as he walked into the room. I loved the smell of my dollar-store shampoo on him.

"That's because it's a kid's towel, but I had to have it." My smile faded and I pulled at the hem of my shorts. "I'm going to shower. It'll only take a few minutes."

He paused picking up his pants. "A woman only taking a few minutes to get ready?"

"Ha-ha," I called as I entered the bathroom. I poked my head back out. "Haven't you realized I'm low maintenance by now?"

∼

Wes

YEAH, I had. I glared at the now shut bathroom door. She'd better shower quickly because as slow as her drain was, she'd overflow the tub within minutes.

Mara had almost talked my dad out of one of his most valuable properties. That old strip mall was in a prime location in Minneapolis. What was her angle? To get a better house? Newer car?

Everyone had a reason motivating their greed. What was Mara's?

If Sam had finalized the paperwork and Mara had become the owner of the building, she could've sold it for millions—to me, because I'd had big plans for the location. The high-end condos and upscale shopping center could make me millions.

The water turned on and I imagined Mara's lithe body under the spray. Blood pooled in my cock and I didn't need to talk another hard-on down.

Her coming on my face. Glorious. I could have her for breakfast, lunch, and dinner.

I shook my head and finished dressing. I liked sex. A lot. But it didn't rule me.

It hadn't *used* to rule me. Since meeting Mara, I could lie in bed all day, fucking her. I had, in fact, except it'd been all night, dotted with a couple hours of sleep before I'd woken with a demanding erection.

My stomach rumbled. As delicious as Mara tasted, she didn't fill my belly. The kitchen I'd glimpsed was opposite of her living room, through a narrow hallway. I shoved my hands in my pockets and went in search of food.

And found myself staring at a short row of cupboards in the smallest kitchen I'd ever experienced. Didn't matter. It's not like I knew how to cook. My sprawling estate employed landscapers, a housekeeper, and a personal chef. They worked during the day when I wasn't around, and when I had the day off, they weren't allowed to show. I liked my privacy.

Besides, my mom would con them and worm her way into my house. And never leave.

She'd eat all my food, too, the trays of five-star meals my chef prepared. Then she'd bitch about it.

Wesley, call your driver to take us to Templeton's. A place she couldn't afford to go on her own. *This food should be trashed. I wouldn't even donate it to the homeless.* As if she ever donated anything.

Wesley, I heard of this fabulous new restaurant in New York. You should fly us there for the weekend. Because being stuck in a plane where I couldn't throw her out was my idea of a fun weekend.

I heard the shower turn off. Shit, Mara was serious about a quick shower.

Cupboards teased me. They were tidy but had seen better days. Probably in the seventies. A couple of cupboard doors were stacked against the wall because they'd fallen off entirely.

Rummaging through her supplies, I decided to give up. Boxes of processed food lined the insides, and cans of sodium-packed whatever filled the rest. Switching to the fridge, I scowled. Milk, Jell-O, and, hallelujah, some fruit.

I pulled out the grapes and milk. Better than nothing and not as toxic as what the cupboards hid. There was a carton of eggs, but hell if I knew what to do with them.

"Oh hey, help yourself." Mara breezed in. "I'll whip up some scrambled eggs. You want any?"

As long as there were no canned veggies in them. "Sure."

I stood, holding the food while I stared at her. She wore black leggings covered in Batman symbols and a yellow top. An outfit that should look immature and ridiculous but didn't on her.

Wet tendrils of hair were piled on her shoulders. It looked like she'd done nothing more than rake a comb through it. She didn't need to do more. With her bangs wet and swept off her face, she radiated youth. No one would guess she was a business owner in her mid-twenties.

She cracked an egg and it nudged me into action, which was to plop my handful of grapes on her tiny, square table. Glasses. I could get those. Did I need to do anything else for grapes?

Her butt jiggled delightfully as she whisked the goop in the bowl. "After I eat, I need to get to the hospital. Do you want me to drop you off somewhere?"

I sat on a chair I wasn't sure would hold my weight. "We can do the same thing we did the other night. I'll call my driver."

She whipped around to look at him. "You have a *driver*?"

I froze, my mind spinning. "No, no. The Uber driver."

Turning back to her eggs, she chuckled. "I was gonna say, those sales must be good."

They were, and it was none of her business. "Tell me about your mom. How's she really doing?"

Mara's shoulders tightened as she stirred the eggs around the skillet. "She has multiple sclerosis."

"What's that exactly?" I'd heard of it, knew it was a disease, probably had seen various fundraising stuff cross my desk for it.

"An autoimmune disorder that attacks the nervous system. For Mom, it started in her thirties. Weird numbness in her hands and feet, her vision would get wonky. Doctors' visits. She carted me along. It was just her and I."

Where was her dad? Another nasty divorce where the father hadn't stuck around?

I couldn't afford to feel sympathy toward her. Mara was no better than my mother, going after Sam for money. But, in many other ways, Mara was way better than my gold-digging, heartless mom. I hadn't witnessed one rude comment from Mara, not to someone's face, not behind their back. Mara's possessions were cared for, even if they weren't high-end. My mother blasted through clothing and jewelry for the sake of her image.

But then Sam probably hadn't seen that side of her when he'd first met her, either.

Mara kicked a foot against her leg and stirred. "When we found out what the cause was, we thought, okay, we can do this. Some people live a full life for decades."

My breath stalled. The rest of her story wasn't going to be good.

"But her relapses grew more frequent, more debilitating. Treatment helped, but eventually, she grew so disabled I couldn't take care of her by myself. She can barely walk." She clicked off the stove and pulled out a couple of plates.

The patterns didn't match. Who had mismatched dishes?

Eggs were piled onto his plate. She plucked some grapes out for each of us.

"Voila." She sat in the chair opposite me, tension dulling her eyes.

"Where does she live then?" I should quit asking. Her mom's health obviously bothered her, and I no longer doubted her mom was really in the hospital.

"A nursing home one of my customers recommended. It's been excellent for Mom. Her health is better with routine care and a steady diet."

We ate in silence. I thought of my mother and how she'd kill herself before she allowed me to put her into a home. She threatened suicide all the time. I suspected she thought of new and unique ways to off herself. The typical ways people killed themselves would be too gauche for Jennifer Robson.

Dehydrate herself and sit hours in the spa's sauna. Fabricate a parasailing accident in the Bahamas. Pufferfish poisoning. Crushed by a rack of designer clothing.

It'd be in a way that wouldn't appear to be her fault. People would utter *that poor woman* and talk about her for weeks, months if my mom planned it right. If she wasn't in therapy, I'd be more concerned her comments were more than a ploy to control me.

"What do your parents do?" Mara's question was hesitant. Was she searching for family money?

My mom is a viper who lives off of whoever will feed her gourmet handouts. "My dad passed away and my mom...does whatever. We're not close."

Sympathy filled her gaze, but it didn't make me uncomfortable. It wasn't the *I'm sorry your dad wanted nothing to do with you and passed away* look. Or the *poor kid left with the batshit crazy mother* one. She genuinely felt bad I'd lost the parental lottery.

"I didn't know my dad." She shrugged and stabbed at her eggs. "Sperm donor."

"I feel like you're fortunate. To know your dad and then

lose him…it's hard." I wasn't talking about Sam's death, either. Going from spending all weekend playing games, watching movies, and hanging out to almost zero contact hit a kid where it hurt. I didn't know what I'd done wrong, what my mother had done that was so horrible a man would cut off his child without explanation. Only as I had gotten older had Sam treated me more like a business partner and probably only because Sam had had no one to leave his empire to.

"I can't imagine how hard it must be. That's what I'm going to experience with Mom and—" She sniffled and pushed back from the table. "Sorry. I don't want to ruin a wonderful morning by bawling. Finish your food. I need to grab a few items before we go."

My appetite was gone. At least I'd eaten most of my food. Her plate was half full, but she carried it to the sink anyway and left.

I picked up my plate and went to set it beside hers, but paused. Should food be left sitting on the counter? It never sat on mine, but all I did was heat my portions. Ms. Gibbons took care of the rest and my counters sparkled when she was through. And my kitchen sink didn't leak like Mara's.

Locating the garbage, I dumped the remnants and went in search of her.

I found her in the only other room of the house I hadn't been in. Another square room, only with superhero posters lining the walls. Mara was sifting through the DVDs lining a shelf.

"Got a thing for Batgirl?"

She spun around with a gasp. "For a big guy, you move quietly."

Four disk cases lay in a pile and a portable DVD player was at her feet.

"Wouldn't a tablet be easier to cart around and watch

movies on?" I wandered around the room, studying the posters.

"Yes, but these are already purchased and I can send them back to the nursing home with her."

Why didn't her mom have her own tablet with movies on it? They only cost a few hundred dollars.

Her cupboards were full of cheap food and the house barely broke four digits in square footage. A few hundred dollars meant more to Mara than to me. I could go out and buy all the tablets sold in the Twin Cities and not even flinch, yet Mara couldn't afford one.

For the first time, I felt a twinge that I'd done something wrong. My bottom line wouldn't miss the strip mall that much, and I'd recover the loss with my other endeavors quickly enough. The tenants who'd move into the high-end condo I had planned would be financially well-off whether or not I built them a luxury home, but Mara would be out of an income stream. And that not only affected her but her mother.

But that was how women like Mara worked. Prey on men's sympathies, tug their heartstrings. I shook myself out of my musings. I wasn't responsible for Mara's financial decisions and I'd never condone conning hard-working people out of their property.

"As for Batgirl," Mara retrieved her items and dropped them into a tote, "this used to be my old room and I was all about girl power growing up."

"Explains Supergirl, too." I indicated the other poster hanging up.

"Exactly." She flashed me a smile and I saw the impish little girl who used to envision herself in powerful female superheroes.

"Then why Star Wars?" I indicated the disks she'd packed.

"Remember, I'm named after Mara Jade Skywalker."

I broke out in a grin. "You, too. I was named after—"

Whoa. I'd almost said my real name.

Her head tilted as she waited for me to finish.

"Uh, I lost my train of thought. I can't remember the story of where I got my name, but it wasn't from Star Wars." Star Trek and I didn't dare say even that. She was smart enough to connect the dots. Named after a Trek character, a rich guy in sales with a driver, and a dad who'd recently passed away. Had Sam ever told her he'd named his son after Wesley Crusher from *The Next Generation*?

"Sam. Hmm." She tapped her chin. "I can't think of where that could be from, either. I'd have to know your parents' tastes. Lord of the Rings? Samwise Gamgee, perhaps?"

My parents' tastes had been wildly different. Why my mom hadn't insisted on naming me Bentley or Tommy Hilfiger, I couldn't guess. Maybe Jennifer had loved Sam once.

"Before we get going, do you want to go out one night this week?" What did people do on real dates? My dates knew sex was all I was interested in, but I needed to see Mara again—but not at work. Would she keep storming into my office building, demanding a meeting?

Her eyes brightened. "Sure. Catch a movie or something?"

The way she hung onto the tote, gripped in front of her in both hands, she looked so girlish and full of hope. Like she thought this might be a relationship that was going somewhere. On my end, nothing had changed. I wanted answers —why Sam? Had she targeted him from the beginning? Had her run-in with my dad at the convention truly been a coincidence? Had the location of her comic book shop been a calculated move because she'd known a single old man owned the place?

"What movie?" I hadn't been to one in years. Sometimes,

Flynn came over to watch a show in my home theater, but it was rare for us to have time off together.

"I've been wanting to see the new Avengers."

I cocked an eyebrow and scanned her posters. "A DC girl wants to go to a Marvel movie?"

"It's my job." She started for the door and I followed her out to the car. "Have you ever been into Arcadia?"

"I haven't. My work doesn't take me by there too often." I almost went as far as saying I'd never heard of Arcadia, but I'd been obsessed with it since going through my father's documents after he died. The lie would be too easy to slip up on. Until my father's passing, that whole strip mall had been nothing but an eyesore I couldn't believe Sam had hung onto.

She tossed me the keys. "You'll have to stop by so I can show you around before it closes."

"I think I will." For the satisfaction of seeing her clearing her shelves and filling packing boxes.

CHAPTER 7

ara

I BLASTED the display case with cleaner. If it weren't for the fact that 60 percent of the clientele were grown-ass men, I'd swear fifteen preschoolers had been pawing the glass.

I scrubbed the greasy prints off and blew a pink bubble half the size of my head with my gum. It made the most satisfying smack when it popped.

"Good one." Chris, my only employee, was sorting and organizing titles behind me.

"Thank you."

We were both subdued. I'd just had the shut-down talk with him before we opened.

I eyed my work. Stalling, that's what I was doing.

"I guess I'd better go make those signs." I straightened and wrapped my arms around myself. My store wasn't chilly, but a gray cloud hung over me now when I was in it. No more orders. No more excitement about opening more days, hiring more workers, thinking of new ways to expand and stock, and broaden our services.

"Mara." Chris shoved a comic into a box. He must be upset. He never mistreated a comic book.

I studied him while I waited for him to continue. Normally, he could pass for late twenties, with his rich brown eyes and shaggy blond hair, but his pensive expression aged him until he looked every day of his thirty-seven years.

Still not old, but not the guy who normally came to work with the enthusiasm of a seven-year-old.

He stared hard at the box in front of him, his hands settled on his hips. "Would you mind if I did some checking?"

"On what?"

If Chris wanted to check on something, I'd let him. He was only the third person I'd ever hired, but he was fantastic. Smart, organized, knowledgeable, responsible. The two employees before him had possessed one or two of those traits. No application had been required for Chris. He'd come in to shop, we'd gotten to talking, he'd wanted a lower-stress job—boom. Employee of the year.

"I still know some people on the city council. One of my good friends is in zoning and planning. Let me talk to her." He blew out a breath and raised his gaze.

"Still know? You used to work for the city?"

He nodded. "I was on the council, but life got in the way. I finished my term and had to step back. Anyway, it's a long shot, but it wouldn't hurt to ensure Mr. Robson has the permits he needs."

Don't get my hopes up. "Because he's planning housing along with a new retail center?"

Chris bobbed his head. "With his money, I'm sure his people know what they're doing, but what-if?"

Yeah, what-if?

The door dinged and Ephraim breezed in. "Hey, guys."

I mustered a smile for Ephraim.

He slowed and glanced back and forth between me and Chris. "Y'all okay? There's a heavy vibe in here."

Chris looked at me, waiting for my lead. I explained everything to Ephraim, including the almost-papers that would've handed me the mall.

"So the three stores in this place, Arcadia, New Treads, and McGuilley's Drink have to shut down or find new locations." Shaking my hair out of my face, I continued. "I can't afford to relocate, so Arcadia's doors are closing."

Chris's brows shot up. "What about if you and I went into business together?"

My heart slammed, then raced as if the men had backed me into a corner. I covered my reaction with a sad smile. "Thanks for the offer, but I put everything I could spare into this place. The rest is dedicated to medical bills. You could strike out on your own."

As much as I liked Chris, a partnership with any man would give him the chance to use me again. Not enough capital and he'd have the upper hand. If I ran into problems with my mom again and Chris had to take over, what would I have to do to get my share of the store back?

We need to talk about your grades, Mara. You can't complete your degree without this class and you mentioned not being able to afford another semester. Let's go to my office and talk.

Chris wasn't my college professor, but I hadn't allowed myself enough therapy to go into business with him. Being a business owner was more than a professional endeavor, it was survival. Sam Robson had almost restored my faith that a man could have an authoritative role over me and not abuse it, but his son had torn it back down.

At least Wesley Robson wasn't degrading my body while he did it.

Chris's face fell, but his expression turned contemplative. "If I did open my own place, I would pick your brains for advice. But I wouldn't move forward unless you were sure you couldn't reboot Arcadia."

"That's considerate, but I need to think about what I want to be when I grow up." Get a job. Have a boss. I'd look for a female boss. But what if the female supervisor was replaced by a male?

Ugh. I might have to kick in a few bucks for a couple more therapy sessions before I started interviewing.

During our exchange, Ephraim hadn't said a word. Nor had he moved. His intent brown eyes were narrowed on nothing. "How close was Sam to completing the paperwork to give you this building?"

Mara frowned. "No clue. He was going to sell it to me, actually. For a dollar."

Ephraim's eyes flared wide. "You could file a lawsuit against Robson Industries for falling through on the deal. If he told his closest advisors about his plans and reasoning, just maybe the judge would be sympathetic."

"That'd cost a fortune." Chris's dubious expression had to match my own. "And it's almost guaranteed she'll lose."

My heart ached at the loss. Sam would've been so disappointed my store didn't survive.

"Sam loved this place." My voice was almost a whisper.

"Why?" Ephraim's eyes were bright. "Did he tell you? It's the why that matters most."

I clamped down before I said why. Guessing only from what Sam had said, it was because of his son and what had gone down during the ugly divorce, and I wasn't the person to fling dirty laundry in public.

"He didn't give me specifics. I think it reminded him of better times, and he sympathized with my situation."

Ephraim waved it off. "We'll be a pest regardless. As for

the cost, let me approach my firm about taking it on pro bono."

My eyes widened and I stepped back. "No, I couldn't."

He'd grown to be my friend, and I knew he was a lawyer, but not that he was the top dog of a law office. Ephraim and Chris were not Dr. Johannsen, and I couldn't let another man's actions define theirs. Besides, they were more like surrogate brothers, like my old friend Sam had been a father figure. But being beholden to a man sent fear racing through me. And what about Ephraim's job?

I shook my head. "Wouldn't angering Wesley Robson be a bad career move for you and the lawyers you work with?"

His expression hardened. "Keeping greedy people like him in check is exactly what my firm's objective is. Did you hear about New York?" At their blank looks, he continued. "He had eight people arrested and rumor has it, he's in a bidding war for the property next door. I hope someone's richer than him, otherwise he'll control that whole neighborhood."

Chris snapped his fingers. "Is that the place with the low-end housing? He has big plans to revamp the neighborhood. No one currently residing there could afford to live there anymore."

Ephraim turned a beseeching look on me. "I'd love to say I have altruistic goals, but it'd be a career-high if I could raise Wesley Robson's blood pressure. That man has more money and power than he deserves."

I contemplated my options. Do nothing or go down swinging. How much would I owe Chris and Ephraim? They had both offered to help. I could walk away at any time. But I wouldn't. I might not have a leg to stand on, but I didn't need to make it easy.

Wes

I STOOD, glaring out the window of my office. Arcadia had two cars parked in front of it. The shoe store had just as many and the pub didn't open until the evening. What had Sam been thinking, letting that place stand?

"It would seem we have a slight problem with one of the permits."

I spun around to face Franklin.

Unperturbed, Franklin pushed his glasses up and refocused on the documents in front of him. "It's a minor matter, but it may push the demo date back."

I snorted. I didn't care. Arcadia had to evacuate in less than five weeks regardless. "You've taken care of all involved?"

"I have. There will be fees."

A hazard of the business. "What's the rest, Franklin?"

My somber assistant had been especially subdued all morning. If Franklin weren't the best at what he did, and trustworthy, I wouldn't have kept him on. For something to bother Franklin, it bothered me—only if it was about work.

Franklin sighed and folded his hands. "I've been contacted by a legal firm. Johnson, Harwood, and Crest have launched a lawsuit against Robson Industries about the unresolved sale of the Heart of Downtown Mall."

My head spun. Unresolved sale. Sam had been planning to give it away. For a dollar. "That's absurd."

I'd been in danger of softening toward Mara and now she was *suing* me? Not seeing her for four days messed with my mind, like I was in withdrawal from her addictive taste. Her body rocked me only because of the deceptive game she was playing. Franklin's news had reminded me of that, and tonight's movie date with her took on new meaning.

Franklin adjusted his glasses, a tic often preceding bad news. "It is absurd. However, it might give a judge pause."

"But it's missing his signature." Incredulous, I stormed back to the window. Nothing had changed at Arcadia. "How the fuck is she paying for this? She lives in a hovel."

Franklin cleared his throat. "You've seen her place?"

If I told Franklin what I was doing, would the guy stay with me? Would he notify Mara? I couldn't tell Franklin. Despite his loyalty, something about my assistant's dismay unsettled me.

Why? My mom would fist-bump me. Then she'd interfere and ruin it. She'd become Mara's worst nightmare. It'd be like high school on 'roids. Name-calling. Shunning, though who Mara had in her inner circle to shun her, I didn't know. Plus, that'd be the end of enjoying Mara's company—no. Her body. I was enjoying the sex, that was all.

Why should I care again? If I wanted the ultimate revenge, I'd spill to my mom that Mara might play me for his money. Mara was already making a move to finish what she'd started with Sam with her silly lawsuit.

I schooled my expression to one of professional calm before I spun around. "I learned everything I could about the new woman after Sam's money."

"It wasn't like that."

"How do you know?" I held my breath as if I waited for a damn good reason, one that would shine a clean light on Mara.

My assistant hesitated a moment. "I don't, but I knew Sam. He wasn't romantically involved with anyone after his first heart attack."

Hopes crashed and I cursed myself. I curled my lip toward Franklin. "Did you hang out, chat about your hookups?"

Franklin's lips pursed. He shuffled the reports, arranged

them neatly, and stuffed them into his briefcase. "I'll find out everything I can about their claim and whether it'll affect our timeline further."

Somehow Franklin brought out the worst in me like he was Sam's conscience lingering on earth.

"What was it?" My voice dropped low, not quite in apology. "What was it about her that captivated him?"

Standing and holding his bag, Franklin seemed to correctly read into my question. "I wish I had an answer for you. I do know that when she leased the space for Arcadia, he was delighted." His head inclined toward the monstrosity sitting in a corner of the office. "Perhaps it was just nostalgia. Have a good day, sir."

Left alone, I faced the pinball machine that had shown up after I'd shut down my dad's offices. Likely Franklin's doing.

For two seconds, I saw myself as a little kid with mussed black hair repeatedly slamming the flippers and earning replay after replay. Bright blue eyes reflecting off the glass that covered an image of a DeLorean, a teenager, and a guy with wild gray hair. The game had been released the same year I had been born. I was surprised I wasn't named Marty instead.

Had the game even been played since the divorce? I had been in and out of Sam's workplace, but after the way Sam had withdrawn from his role as a father, I had concentrated on learning the business.

Stupid machine. I needed to get rid of it. Give it away, like my dad had tried giving all his other property away.

Speaking of giving property away, I palmed my phone from my pocket and punched in a number.

My executive assistant, Helen, answered, anticipating my question. "I'm a mile away. The car is a hybrid, but not top of the line. I made sure to keep the cost under fifty grand and not too flashy."

"Well done."

Going back to my window, I shoved my hands into my pockets. A few minutes later, Helen pulled into my reserved spot with a black, blah vehicle. Nothing about it screamed class or money and it was exactly what I'd need on my date. If I showed up with my Audi, I might not get the honest answers I wanted from Mara. Like how close she and her *good friend* Sam had been.

I should be disgusted, not only at the thought of Mara and my dad but at the forty-year age difference between the two. But Sam was gone and Mara was almost like my last connection to the man—the man, not the corporate tycoon.

My phone buzzed. Withdrawing it, I saw a text from Helen, giving me details on the movie I planned to take Mara to.

A lawsuit. That greedy woman.

The conundrum it created in my mind aggravated me. Was there someone in her life driving her to rob an old man and continue trying even after his heart had failed him? The Mara I'd taken to bed, with the sick mom and the tiny house, wasn't the avaricious Arcadia owner who'd latched onto Sam.

Even my mom had withdrawn her claws from Sam's empire after the funeral. Because I had gotten everything and now she played the part of a doting mother, one she sucked at.

A tap on the door yanked my attention away.

"Come in." I knew it was Helen. She was the only one with free access to the building and didn't need to be buzzed up.

The older woman breezed in, her cheeks flush with excitement. A car woman, I'd known to call her when I needed a normal car for my date. If I was inclined, I'd feel sorry for the car salesman. Helen drove a hard bargain and was tenacious as fuck.

Just to hear the story, I made sure to ask. "You got a good deal, I presume."

I didn't care. The cost of the car was pocket change.

She chortled and flopped down in the chair Franklin had vacated. "The guy tried to talk to me like I was a little old lady." Helen pinned me with an amused stare and patted her bun. "It's the reason I don't color my hair. Gray hair equals underestimation and I can eat 'em alive."

It wasn't just the gray hair, but also the extra pounds she carried and the matronly way she dressed. Helen's love of sweets often invaded my office and people stupidly assumed a few extra pounds meant fewer IQ points. She'd been jobless when she'd applied for her current position, having stayed home with her kids until they'd left for college. No CEO would hire her with her lack of experience, age, and "frumpy" appearance.

Idiots. Helen's no-nonsense attitude and razor-sharp intellect were obvious and a refreshing change from the interviewees who'd eyed me like hungry tigers, planning ways they could use me to move up in the business world.

She pulled out her laptop. "Franklin asked if I could go over what's going on with your plans in New York with you."

I chose the seat next to Helen. If Franklin had passed off the project to Helen…it was serious enough to take my mind off Mara.

CHAPTER 8

ara

My house came into view and I frowned.

Was that Sam's car sitting in front?

Dammit, I knew I was running late, but combined with him being early, I groaned. Tonight was supposed to be fun and relaxing. Instead, he was waiting and I looked a hot mess.

Pulling behind him, I paused as he unfolded his long frame from his vehicle.

Fading evening sun glinted off his glossy hair and cast shadows over his hard features. After what we'd done together, I shouldn't get nervous, but the predatory intensity of his gaze set my butterflies on fire. They burned up into ash and I gulped.

He was walking to meet me but the flow of his movements was more like he was stalking me.

Managing to gather my stuff before he opened my door, I

smiled up at him. More fluttering in my belly. His expression said he planned to chew me up, spit me out, and gobble me back down.

I grasped his outstretched hand and he pulled me out.

"Sorry, I'm running late." I'd been locking the door when Ephraim had called. My new lawyer.

He cocked an arrogant eyebrow and crowded me close to the car. "You're not late," he murmured before dropping his head.

My lips parted and met his. I was not in making-out condition. Frazzled, stressed, and dusty from a day of unpacking and relabeling inventory for clearance.

Sam must not mind. His tongue coaxed mine out and if he carried it any further, I'd drop my purse and tote and climb him like I was King Kong and he was the Empire State Building.

I flattened a hand on his chest and pushed myself back. His gaze sharpened, dipped down to my lips.

How badly did I want to see that movie?

If this thing between us had a chance, hiding for sex marathons wasn't going to allow it to grow.

And I really wanted something between us. Not because he was a fifteen out of ten on the hotness scale. Because I felt comfortable around him. None of my quirks gave him pause, he'd been helpful while Mom was sick, and I felt sexually free with him like I hadn't felt in years, or ever.

I hadn't realized how important that was. It was a sign that my past didn't rule me.

I mentally sighed. Must also mean I should start filling out applications.

He was still staring at me, waiting for me to make a move.

"I need to get changed."

Stepping back, he held up the hand he still clutched and twirled me. I released a giggle.

"Look good to me." He spun me back into him.

Faded jeans and a *Suicide Squad* tee sounded like a little black dress in his voice.

"I want fresh clothes. I worked hard for the money today."

"All right." He released my hand and draped an arm around my shoulder as he steered me to the door. "Got any more of those leggings?"

The grin that grew lifted the whole week of stress. "Pick your DC superhero."

He grimaced. "I've got bad news, Mara Jade. I was always more of a Marvel guy and I've already seen you in Iron Man."

I gasped dramatically and elbowed him playfully. "I don't know if this thing between us will work." Letting us into my place, I dropped my things by the door. "Lucky for you, I run a place where I have to be a well-rounded fangirl. I'll be right back."

No looking back as I trotted to my room or I'd never leave the house. I swung the bedroom door shut and unsnapped my pants.

The door didn't latch and I glanced back. Sam towered in my doorway, his expression even more severe than earlier. My breath hitched.

"Go ahead." His guttural tone liquefied me. "Drop your pants."

"The movie?" It was all I could think of saying.

"We have forty-five minutes. Drop your pants and crawl back on the bed." He reached for his wallet and withdrew a square packet.

Sucking in my lower lip, more with excitement than trepidation, I shucked my pants off, taking my panties at the same time. Doing as he ordered, I scooted back onto the mattress.

He freed himself from his black jeans, doing nothing

more than lifting his polo out of the way, unsnapping his pants, and shoving them and his underwear under his shaft.

The condom was rolled on within seconds and he pushed my legs apart. I fell back.

He slid a finger through my crease. "You're wet for me."

No answer. My voice didn't work. His cock replaced his finger and he shoved inside. I cried out as he groaned and dropped his head.

"Been too long," he said between gritted teeth.

He took full control, backed out, and thrust again, harder. My hands flew to his shoulders, splaying against the soft fabric covering hard muscle.

His pace increased until he pounded me. Circling my clit with his thumb, his hips pistoned until I gasped with the rising climax. He went faster. The seams of his jeans cut into my thighs, his shirt tickling my abdomen.

My hands twisted into his polo, my back arching upon my surrender.

A snarl of emotion left him as he growled out his orgasm, grinding together with mine.

Raw sex. Fast and hard. I'd never experienced anything like it, but with Sam, I'd had a lot of firsts.

Pulling out, he stepped back and headed for the door without looking back. "Now, I'll wait where you told me to."

The door was pulled closed behind him and I was left with a delicious ache in my body but a thread of confusion blooming in my heart.

∼

Wes

. . .

I BRACED my hands on Mara's bathroom counter. I'd stripped off the condom and locked my dick back up where it belonged. My heart raced, had been since my skin had touched Mara while helping her out of her car.

Two minutes and I couldn't keep away from her. Who could blame me? Her T-shirt was a solid size too small. Did customers notice how it molded around her breasts? As good as a marquis. The way her hips rolled as she walked to her bedroom. I'd been half-hard in anticipation of Mara's body all day, but the reality of her was too much for my sex drive.

My plan wasn't going to work if I fell under her spell. Soon, I'd be signing over building after building to her just to keep her in my bed.

Shooting myself a disgusted look in the mirror, I exited the bathroom and shut the door so I didn't have to listen to the constant drip of the sink. Reclining against her front door, I waited.

Her house was seriously cramped. How was she affording a team of lawyers? Didn't she have her mom's hospital bills? We'd texted all week and her mom had gone back to the nursing home Monday. What about that bill?

I'd have Franklin look into how much a month at Golden Meadows cost. In fact, I'd have Franklin—no. Helen. She would comb through Mara's history with ruthless precision as soon as I said the word. Helen was more territorial of me than my mother. Maybe it was job security for my executive assistant, but I didn't often question it.

Having someone give a shit about me personally was refreshing.

Was that why Mara crawled under my skin, sent blood screaming toward my cock with her smile and fresh scent?

She blew out of the bedroom, her sex-flushed cheeks sending another flow of blood to my privates.

"What's that scent you wear?" I blurted. God, maybe I

should go home until I had my thinking straight. Ending my day with the PR mess in New York didn't help.

"Just washed?" she drawled.

"You don't wear perfume?"

She chuckled. "It's called dollar-store fabric softener." Her smile faded when she caught my expression. "Are you okay?"

"Bad day at work."

"Ah. I get it."

After I settled her into my new car, I climbed in. She was looking around the interior. "Geez, this thing is immaculate. And it still has that new car smell."

"I've had it for a while." I may have fudged and put my other car's plates on this one to make it look that way. I didn't want to explain a new car and didn't want her to reveal her greedy side so soon. Well, I did, that was the whole point of dating her, but maybe after the movie. It'd been a long time since I'd done something as normal as going to a movie. Here's to hoping I didn't get pulled over for anything. "How's closing your place going?"

I drove to the theater and let Mara go on about learning how to shut down a business.

"The best part of the week was when one of my loyal customers offered to represent me pro bono on the incomplete contract my friend Sam left behind."

I had to mentally scream at myself to not stomp on the brake. Pro bono? She'd conned one of her customers enough to represent her *for free*?

What had she done for him to manage that?

I almost snarled.

"Sam, are you sure you're okay?"

I forced a smile. "Sorry, my attitude's stuck at work, but not my attention. Keep going."

The little crinkle in her forehead was too cute for words. I redoubled my efforts to remain emotionally distant. She'd bamboozled my dad and her customers, and I hadn't figured out what she wanted out of him.

"I had to put up a notice that my store's closing in five weeks, barely over a month. They were upset, understandably so. I mean, we're like a small family. Chris offered to contact an old friend on the city commission."

A proprietary swell rose. "Who's Chris?"

"My full-time employee. My only employee, really. He left his career for something more mellow. Best thing that ever happened to my store. Anyway, Ephraim overheard—he's a customer—and they started talking. I turned him down at first. I don't think there's a chance, but…" She shrugged and flashed me a mischievous smile. "There's nothing wrong with being a pain in Wesley Robson's ass."

I ground my molars together. PITA, all right. My lawyers would fall over laughing at the thought of pro bono work.

"That's a stroke of luck," I said instead.

Her smile faded. "I've been fortunate to be surrounded by decent people these last few years."

And before that? She could be attempting to tug at my heartstrings, to build my curiosity in her. Working on the fragile-woman-needing-protection angle.

To be honest, I had a hard time seeing a fragile woman who needed to be cared for. Mara was ambitious and independent.

She didn't elaborate on her past. This would've been the perfect time to dive into a sob story, but she remained mum.

I could still get my own information out of her. "What's their plan?"

She waved her hand. "I don't know all the legal wording. Mostly Sam's intention to sell the place to me was a transaction involving Robson Industries. It wasn't finalized, but there may be some loopholes because it was the company or at least a way to delay the stupidity. I don't know. I keep thinking I could talk some sense into Sam's son and this might give me time, or bring him out of the mysterious meetings he's always in when I call."

That it might do. "A dollar. How do the other tenants in the mall feel?"

The movie theater was a block away and I was finally getting some answers.

"I don't know that they'd care as long as it was run the same. I wasn't planning on kicking them out so I could sell it. I just wanted to keep Arcadia open."

I parked but made no move to get out. "An old man sells a young woman prime realty for a dollar and you don't think they'd mind?"

It'd taken a lot of effort to keep the scorn out of my voice.

She frowned at me. "It's not like Sam and I were anything more than friends, so I don't really care what they'd think."

Nothing more than friends. A helluva favor my dad had been doing a *friend*.

A delicate eyebrow cocked. "Are we going inside?"

I softened my features, but they didn't match my roiling emotions. "It's a Marvel movie. Are you really in a rush?"

Her laughter delighted me when I should be seething. "Trust me. Any loyalties are suspended when it comes to blockbuster movies."

I walked with her into the theater. Flashes of my childhood bombarded my mind as soon as the popcorn aroma swamped me. Every weekend, Sam would take me to the movies, and not just to escape my mother. It was our bonding time. Legit time together and an activity we both loved. If there wasn't a new movie out, we went to an old one. Sam had even looked into purchasing a theater or even building a new one.

Then my mom had struck. Whether it was jealousy or pure manipulation, she'd made sure to be caught *en flagrante* with Sam's realtor. As a kid, I had blamed the other man for the marriage's demise, but as an adult, I recognized my mother's machinations. No man was stupid enough to drop trou and get head in his most lucrative client's office.

As I sat for the movie, I asked the question that'd plagued me for over a decade. My mom. The realtor. Mara. Had Sam been gullible his whole life? The only person in Sam's life not out to use him had been me and he'd dumped me a hot second after the divorce.

CHAPTER 9

es

I STARED DUBIOUSLY at the clothes Helen had picked up at my request. Bless the lady, she hadn't batted an eye.

It'd been a good idea at the time.

I have plans to take Mom to the TC Comic-Con this Saturday. Want to go? You get a discounted entrance if you dress up. Mom always goes as Leia from Star Wars. I'm going to dig out an old Batgirl costume. Wanna come?

The red jacket with black shoulders and black slacks didn't taunt me so much as the Star Trek com badge.

I'd been out of my damn mind when I'd agreed. Dress up?

The line of thought I'd run away with was that I could dress like Wesley Crusher and get a little satisfaction from being Wesley when accompanying her as Sam.

Walking around in a costume didn't drum up anxiety like meeting her mother, however. Not just meeting her, but busting her out of the home and carting her all over town.

Give her sick mother an afternoon to remember before bringing her back... No pressure.

I jumped into the shower only because I needed wet hair to slick over like I remembered on the character from the show, but it'd been many, many years since I'd watched it.

Satisfied with my appearance, I thought I looked more like Number One, Captain Picard's first officer, with his black hair, but there weren't enough pips on my collar for the rank of commander. Besides, that crowd would *know* who I was.

I packed an overnight bag and headed to Mara's. She was driving because she knew how to load the wheelchair in her car and didn't want to find out my trunk wasn't as chair friendly. Her offer to pick me up was dissuaded by me plainly telling her I was overnighting.

No way could she see my obnoxious house. She'd know I was no normal sales dude when she drove up to my multi-million-dollar mansion.

I parked in my normal spot and trotted up to her door, feeling *ridiculous* in a costume. Twenty years ago it had been a different story.

All thoughts vanished when Batgirl answered the door wearing knee-high, shiny black boots, and a miniskirt that allowed a peek of thigh. I'd grown used to her baggy shirts, so the yellow utility belt cinched at her waist induced fantasies about what our sleepover would entail.

"Wesley Crusher! Awesome. I love costumes that are a little more obscure." She grabbed her mask and stepped out.

I found my tongue. "Aren't you cold?"

"I've got a cape." She grinned and sashayed away.

We climbed into her car and she backed out. "You know what you'll have to do? The Picard Maneuver."

"Excuse me?"

"Every time you stand up, pull the front of your jacket down."

Yeah, I remembered the move, but leave it to Trekkies to give it a name.

"I don't want to break character."

She laughed, but our banter didn't break up the case of nerves I'd suddenly developed. I had a vague idea of where Golden Meadows was and the closer we got, the more my hands trembled.

"What's your mom's name again?"

"Wendy." She glanced at me, at the road, then back at me. "You sure you're okay with this?"

"Of course, but come on, it's meeting the mom."

She smiled and her next words seemed timid. "I'm sure I'd feel the same way if I met yours."

"I wouldn't do that to you." And I wouldn't, no matter how much resentment and suspicion I harbored.

She sobered and turned her gaze back out the window.

"It's not you, Mara. She's…a different creature. Doesn't make people feel good about themselves."

"I understand." She didn't sound like it.

A sprawling brick building with timber framework came into view. With startling honesty, I determined my place was bigger.

"Are they ready for us?" I meant to lighten the mood, but I didn't know if that was more for myself than her.

Meeting a parent. I'd known dates' parents from my social circle. But dressed for Comic-Con? That was a first.

"They'll love it."

I followed in her wake as she smiled at the staff that randomly appeared from offices and residents' rooms. She waved to other residents as they meandered by, some with no assistance, many in wheelchairs, and a smattering of walkers. I nodded in greeting. Mara was right, they enjoyed the show.

We turned into a sunny, quiet room where a thin woman who looked no younger than my mom waited in a wheelchair. Wendy Baranski had hair a similar color as Mara's natural hue, only with a sprinkling of gray. Her eyes radiated kindness but were wary as if every day was a struggle.

"Are you all set, Mom? Oh, we have to do your hair." Mara went straight for a narrow closet door but stopped before she dove inside. "Mom, this is Sam."

Her mom smiled and held out a frail hand for a shake. "Nice to meet you. Call me Wendy."

"Likewise, Wendy." I grasped her hand lightly. Wendy's skin was soft and warm with more strength than I expected, but when I let go, the subtle tremor of her hand returned.

Several things ran through my mind, but all sounded like inane dribble. I talked up girls at my club, prospective buyers and sellers, and my friends during a few get-togethers. But I'd never…just chatted, not without an agenda. Wendy wasn't the guys I hung out with, neither was she Franklin or Helen, not that I small-talked those two.

Wendy's gentle smile eased my case of what-do-I-say. "Have you been to TC Comic-Con before?"

"It's been a while. I don't believe I've ever been in a costume as an adult."

She chuckled. "This is an annual tradition for Mara and I, as long as I'm up for it."

"Found it." Mara popped out of the closet. In her hands was a wig with stereotypical Princess Leia buns and a draping white dress.

"I'll step out." I scurried around the corner, but instead of hiding, I'd made myself the center of attention.

A young nurse's aide walked by with a demure smile,

gazing at me under hooded eyes. Her hips kicked out more as she passed me. An older aide trailed behind her, but her look had a maternal quality that I rarely saw in my own mother.

"You two look delightful," she said as she charged past Wendy's room.

I threw her a "thanks" and nearly jumped out of my threads when an elderly man spoke behind me.

"Busting Wendy out of here today, eh?" The man's wizened hands leaned on his metal walker.

"Yes, sir."

A grin lifted the man's wrinkled face. "Good. Good. Too young to be stuck with us old people. You kids have fun."

"You as well."

He shuffled off.

Was Mara able to bust Wendy out of here often?

After the convention, I could treat us all to dinner. Even if Mara was trying to use me, the simple cost of a meal was nothing. I'd be starving and convention snacks wouldn't tide me over. And…we were busting Wendy out of a pretty boring place. I wasn't in a rush to bring her back.

Mara wheeled a giddy Wendy out into the hallway.

"Do I need to bring the car up front?" I asked.

Mara lifted a shoulder without removing her hand from the handles of the chair. "There's no snow so the parking lot is no issue. They tend to make the parking spots wider here. Kinda nice."

Exiting was the same as entering. Mara and Wendy were wished well by nearly everyone they passed. Did the whole facility know?

I sat in the backseat. Mara had offered to let me drive, but the idea of sitting up front with her mother must be what my staff experienced before a board meeting.

Oh god, what do I say? What's she going to say? How do I respond?

Plus the back had the added bonus of watching the profile of a pink-haired Batgirl.

"Mom, can you get the handicap parking pass from the glove compartment?"

A task that should've taken seconds took a few solid minutes as Wendy worked the latch, dug the pass out, closed the cubby, and hung the pass up.

I glanced at my own hands, so strong and competent, then at Mara's young and healthy body. A new respect for Wendy bloomed.

What Mara had tried to do to Sam wasn't okay, but…it was more understandable.

As she found a spot to park, I stared at everyone walking by. I might've stood out anywhere in Minneapolis, but here, I was the norm. Underdressed even, as every superhero imaginable, aliens, monsters, and other unidentifiable creatures strode by. When I turned forward, Mara had donned her facemask.

More fantasies about what the night entailed.

Again, Mara sent my gold-digger radar off-kilter when she produced three tickets as we entered the convention center.

Sam had brought me here when I was a kid, but I still looked around with the wonder of an eight-year-old boy. Things had grown—on a much larger scale, with more variety. Costumes ranged from furry to cosmic to barely there. Many were obviously handmade or thrown together. Several people walked by in getups that must've cost hundreds of dollars. The age range of attendees varied more than I remembered. Every age was represented and groups roamed, either families or college-aged kids, along with a ton of couples.

I smirked. *The couple that dresses up together stays together?*

"It's something, isn't it?" Mara whispered as we wandered

shoulder to shoulder.

She pushed Wendy, whose grin was infectious to all who passed.

"So what are your plans?" I tried to remember what me and Sam used to do. Panels, new toys, shows, there had to be all that and then some now.

"We mostly walk around. It's the costumes that are our favorite."

I had to tell Flynn about this shit. Because while Mara's costume was sexy as hell, there were women aplenty who strutted by in barely-there costumes. My friend would tear through the convention and leave with triple digits in phone numbers, and maybe a quick hookup in a secluded spot.

"Oh look, Mom. That guy with the vintage action figures is here again." Mara plowed through the crowd, apparently unafraid of using her mom's chair in the same manner the prow of a ship cut through water.

She talked excitedly with her mom as they perused old merchandise that had never been removed from its box. I hung toward the edge, more than mildly interested but not wanting to show it.

The booth next to the action figures was fan art and I went over for a look.

Two women were whispering next to me. Their giggles drifted over the din.

Weren't they cold in those outfits? One wore full-body spandex in powder blue. No clue who she was supposed to be. The other was in black spandex with holes randomly torn through, mostly across her rounded butt cheeks.

Flynn would love this.

Mara glanced over toward me, then bent to speak to Wendy. As I was turning away to meet up with them, one of the girls called to me.

"Wes?"

My eyes widened and my feet stalled. The floor could be wet concrete for as well as my legs worked. My right eye twitched.

"Wes, right?" Her pitch rose in excitement.

Mara had noticed the exchange, her glance going between me and the girls.

I pivoted back and pointed to the small, round pip on my collar. "Yes, Wesley Crusher. Good eye."

The ass-less girl stepped toward me, her mouth stretched in a seductive grin. "No, not Cr—"

My sharp glare made her smile falter.

"Don't you remember me, from my friend's"—she indicated blue Lycra girl—"bachelorette party…at Canon?"

Aww, damn. If I tried hard, I might remember her.

I kept my demeanor pleasant, didn't sneer like I wanted. She could ruin everything. But it wasn't her fault I thought my partners were nothing more than passing entertainment.

"I'm sorry, but I'm escorting two lovely ladies around today and I must go."

I spun back to Mara as she approached. "What would you like to see next?"

Mara

IT WAS ALL I could do not to stare at the girl with her ass hanging out of her costume. She was sexy and sultry…and incredibly hurt by what appeared to be a brush-off from Sam.

An ex? A former fling?

Current fling?

Whoever she was threw a disgusted look at Sam's back as

she walked away with her friend.

Sam was watching me, waiting for an answer, but I so badly wanted to sate my curiosity.

"Well, there's a huge line where they're giving out swag T-shirts, or I'd give it a try."

My mom raised my face to them. "If we're going to wait in line, we might as well try to get into a panel. Unless you want to walk around and get ideas for Arcadia?"

My eyes shot to Sam, who arched a brow but didn't say anything.

"No, I think there's some interesting panels." I handed the schedule of events to Sam and wove my way out of the exhibition hall.

He was subdued for the rest of the afternoon. No, that wasn't right exactly. He wasn't saying much, but he walked with tight shoulders and scrutinized everyone who sat by us or walked past.

We found seats at a panel of graphic novel artists. Sam sat on one side of me and Mom on the other.

"Is everything okay?" I murmured to him.

"Just thinking about where to take you two for dinner."

My brows shot up. "Oh, you don't have to."

His piercing gaze brooked no argument. "I'd like to."

Dinner out sounded divine and, ordinarily, it'd be a treat, but eating wasn't the easiest for Mom.

I turned to my other side. "Sam wants to take us out for dinner. Would you be okay with that?"

Mom had the same reaction. She wanted to be thrilled, buuut…

"I think I'll be fine, as long as I order something soft like mashed potatoes. The tremors aren't terrible today."

I gauged the truth of her words. She often mentioned how frustrating her meals could be. Many of the foods she loved were too hard, too chewy, or too gooey for her to enjoy anymore. And with her tremors, soup was best sipped out of a cup.

Mom leaned in close. "Are you sure you two wouldn't rather be alone?"

I couldn't fight my grin. "He invited the two of us."

"Well, okay. But you know what I always say."

Don't let him break your heart.

"Can't forget."

After the panel, we exited the convention center. I missed my jacket, but it wouldn't have done much good with the bitter breeze blowing up my skirt.

"Where would you like to go?"

We sat in the idling car and I twisted around. "Where do you usually go?"

His expression froze. Tough question?

"I don't get out much."

I narrowed my gaze on him. Another girl might not question his behavior, but he was acting odd enough to set off my spidey sense.

Giving myself an invisible shake, I brushed it off. Not every male interested in me was deceitful.

Maybe that's why I'd gotten along so well with Sam Robson. Not once had I gotten anything other than a friendly vibe from him.

"I'll drive and Mom can shout out a place she'd like."

Mom chuckled. "Sure, put the pressure on me."

A simple family restaurant won out.

I didn't miss the subtle lift of Sam's forehead when he scanned the menu. He might not get out much, but I was confident that when he did, it wasn't to places like this. With his nice car and sharp clothes, he likely ate at more expensive places.

He ordered seamlessly and as I relaxed to enjoy the meal, I couldn't help but think of how little I knew about him.

CHAPTER 10

es

"And where were you all weekend?" Flynn stepped inside my office at Canon and shut the door. "I gotta wait until Monday night to see my boy. You left me hanging."

I shuffled papers around on my desk and opened a file on my computer. Wrong one. I closed it. I couldn't concentrate until my friend left. Flynn wasn't going to quit until he pried out everything I was willing to share.

"I was kidding, but were you with her *all weekend*? The comic book store owner you're 'fooling'?" Flynn gave the last word air quotes.

I pushed back and crossed an ankle over my knee. "I *am* fooling her. I hung out with her and her mom." Ignoring Flynn's gaping mouth, I continued, "Guess what? She's on such good terms with some of her customers that one is representing her pro bono to contest Sam's contract."

"I'm going to ignore the mother part because, dude, you

don't do family—yours or anyone else's. But the lawsuit? A fool's errand. Why bother?"

"To be a nuisance."

"And you and her are doing what this whole time?"

I didn't answer. I didn't appreciate being put on the spot and I wasn't going to share my sex life with Flynn.

Flynn's eyes narrowed and he huffed. "So you're hooking up. Don't like repeat performances, my ass."

I didn't like repeat performances, they just led to complications. Mara was a special exception. I tapped a pen while Flynn loomed on the other side of my desk. I thought of an answer that wouldn't incriminate me with Flynn.

"I need to know why my dad was so into her."

Flynn gave me the *duh* look. "Why are *you* so into her? Answer that and there's your answer. Have you drawn up any contracts with her name on them lately?"

"Fuck, no."

"Really? *You met her mother.* Prove she doesn't have you brainwashed. Go out there and pick up that blond hot thing that goes by the name of Hailey but doesn't mind what you call her when you're balls deep."

I winced at the...stunning accuracy of what being with Hailey was like. It reminded me of how little I liked *Sam* being screamed when I was buried in Mara.

"I have some work to do."

"She's got you, brother. Finish your work and get out here and show me that Mara Joy Budinski doesn't have a hold on you."

Mara Jade Baranski, asshole.

Flynn left and I scrubbed my face. Stared at my work. All of which would've been done over the weekend, when I usually dealt with club business. It taunted me after a long day in the office because I'd ignored messages over the weekend.

Flynn was right. She was getting to me. I pushed back from my chair and went out to the dance floor.

∼

Mara

I BLEW a bubble and snapped it, the pop echoing through Arcadia. So satisfying.

No one was around. The sweet spot of a Wednesday afternoon, when I got very few customers until people started getting off work.

Since there was no one to impress, I sat behind the register "borrowing" a Justice League comic. Ordinarily, I didn't sample the merchandise but with a little over three weeks left, I was cutting loose. Soon, affording comics would go back to being a luxury.

The door tinkled as a shockingly handsome man in a designer suit and perfectly coiffed hair strolled in. He glanced around with a bemused expression.

I closed the comic and hopped down from my stool. "What are you looking for today?"

I'd learned a long time ago not to ask *What can I do for you today?* when my clientele was predominantly male.

He zeroed in on me like a bird of prey. His gaze swept down my purple plaid flannel shirt to my black Star Wars leggings emblazoned with C-3PO on one leg and R2-D2 on the other.

An arrogant blond brow rose.

So it was like that.

"I just heard about this place. Wanted a look around before it closed." His rich voice probably left a puddle of estrogen wherever he went.

But what was up with the hair? I wanted to tell him that the nineties called and they wanted their frosted tips back. Said the girl with pink hair. Whatever, it worked on him.

As he approached, he didn't look over any of my shelves.

I didn't get nervous often when alone in the store, but my gut began a slow churn. What did this guy want? Was he one of those types that forced himself on a girl because normally they found him irresistible?

Because I could resist him. No way interested. For instance, I liked black hair and sharp blue eyes. A man with an easy grin who harbored an inner fanboy. Sam. I preferred a man like Sam.

I cleared my throat. "Are you looking for comics, graphic novels, games for any specific gaming system?"

He stopped and frowned. "What's the difference between a comic and a graphic novel?"

"There are a few things. Graphic novel storylines don't run for as many issues as comics, so they're longer, and the story tends to be more complicated."

His expression read *Why should I care?*

"We also have a small collection of movies. Have you seen *Deadpool*?"

His unusual gray eyes brightened and he barked out a laugh. "Yeah, I have. Do you sell that here?"

I led him to the movie rack.

He snatched it off the shelf and read the back. I finally relaxed around him because now he was acting like a fanboy. "I'd have to buy a Blu-ray player to watch it. I haven't bought a DVD in years."

It was getting more common these days.

"You know, I saw this in my buddy's home theater." His vivid gaze latched onto mine. "I don't get to hang with him much because he's found a new girl."

Said in a way that sounded like my fault. "Happens."

He leaned in until his smooth-smelling cologne washed over me. A sly smile stretched his lips. "I could find a girl of my own."

"I'm sure it's not hard for you."

He drew back. Was I supposed to fall all over myself?

"Harder than you might think," he muttered and wandered to the register. "I think I'm going to get this."

I rang him up and when he handed me his card, the block letters spelled out *Flynn Halstengard*.

"Do you want to go get a drink sometime?"

As charming as he was, I had no urge to meet him anywhere. "I'm sorry, I'm seeing someone."

He playfully pouted. "Must be a special guy."

"I think so." But I was afraid to give my heart totally to him. If I could at least see where he lived and know more about him, I'd feel better.

"Hope he's turning them away like you are." Flynn smiled, the poster child for a toothpaste commercial, and gave me a wink before he left.

Well...Mr. Flynn Halstengard had certainly set an ominous tone I needed to shrug off. A stranger wasn't going to dictate whether I trusted my new boyfriend or not.

CHAPTER 11

es

ON FRIDAY, Flynn left his fifth voicemail since Monday night.

I blew it off and glared at the strip mall out of my office tower's window. If Sam had torn that eyesore down years ago, none of this would've happened. Mara would've been forced to set up shop somewhere else and probably wouldn't have been able to afford any of my dad's other properties.

She wouldn't have latched onto Sam, and I wouldn't have met her. Wouldn't have gotten to know her. Would their paths have ever crossed?

My office door opened and Flynn barged in.

"Ignoring me much?"

"I don't want to hear it." I turned and waited for Flynn's reproach.

"You need to. Did you even kiss anyone at the club? Rub yourself against them? When Hailey scooted that fine ass of hers into you, you jumped like a fifty-year-old virgin at a swinger's party."

Hailey's painted-on dress and banging body should've been Robson catnip. She was a naturally beautiful girl and wielded her makeup wand like a warrior, turning herself into the stuff of men's fantasies. I had always limited sex with her because she smacked of clinginess. She also gave off *I'll fuck your best friend on your desk* vibes. And while Hailey and Flynn had hooked up, neither me nor my buddy worried about territory issues. No man was idiot enough to try to claim Hailey.

With Flynn's prodding, she'd scooted up to me as soon as I'd stepped out of my office. Probably had been hoping to bang one of us on my desk.

But instead of double-D tits and hips that could swirl the alphabet over my dick, I saw a girl who didn't have her shit together. Instead of blond highlights and lowlights and whatever else women did to their hair, I missed the pink.

And Mara's hips were perfectly capable of alphabet sex.

"I need to see this thing through with Mara, and I need to focus."

"On what? Letting her fuck with you?"

"Enough!"

Flynn's mouth snapped shut.

Ah, hell. She was driving a wedge between us.

"What if…just let me find out what was going on between her and Sam." I sunk into the couch in my office. "I'm starting to think, I don't know, that maybe they were just friends and it wasn't about the money. Let me find out why he wanted to spend the time with her that he used to spend with me."

"I see. Coulda said so, dude."

I sputtered.

Flynn shrugged it off and strolled to the pinball machine.

"I get it. I know how Sam bailed on you. You're pissed he was getting his geek on with Mara Jana Baslinski and you're worried it wasn't about the booty."

Flynn was crack on, except for her name. Mara. Jade. Baranski. Fucker.

"Does this thing even work?" Flynn punched the buttons. Nothing happened.

"Probably. If it's plugged in." I snickered and earned the finger. "I doubt you'd even need a quarter. Sam gave everything away." Or sold it for a *dollar*.

Squatting in his pressed slacks, holding his tie in like he was at the edge of a fashion show runway, Flynn fished around for the cord until he hooked it. "Score."

I stood back with my arms folded. The guy was tenacious about the damn game.

I didn't help, but my buddy finally spied the outlet behind the pinball game. Flynn wrestled the machine away from the wall to plug it in.

A muscle flexed in my jaw. My breath stalled. The game lit up like opening night at the Minnesota State Fair.

Flynn released a triumphant *whoop* and assumed the pinball position.

I shook my head. The words *you want it?* hovered on my tongue. Nah. Flynn could play it whenever he stopped in. I would give it away later.

"Ha! Extra balls. *Yasss*." Flynn had developed the wide-legged stance I had often used when I'd wasted his childhood on it. My friend punched the flippers. "So...I went to Arcadia the other day."

"What? Why?" My pulse kicked up. What had Flynn said? What had he done? What had *they* done?

"Relax. Just checking her out. She's cute. The pink hair, plaid shirt, and Star Wars leggings aren't your usual type."

"I told you—"

"Yeah, yeah." He whooped and slapped the machine. "I am the pinball master."

I couldn't bring myself to ask, but I didn't need to. Flynn beat me to it.

"She didn't take the bait, man. Maybe I'm not rich enough, or her eyesight's off and she thinks you're really better looking."

I gave up my eagle perch over Arcadia and glared at Flynn. I sat behind my desk, but my mind was stuck on the Star Wars leggings I hadn't seen yet and how much I legitimately looked forward to our date later that night.

∼

Mara

I SLID into Wes's car. "It's your choice on what to do tonight. I owe you for being such a good sport at Comic-Con last weekend."

Wes kept the car in park, a faraway glaze to his eyes. "What is there to do on a Friday night? I'm usually catching up with work."

"Good question. I'm usually playing my Xbox. I mean," I gave him a sly smile, "testing new games so I can give proper sales advice. Or watching a movie."

"Gaming sounds fun, but I want to be active."

His heated stare made me want to strip down in the car.

I grinned, a flush blooming on my cheeks. "Active is nice, but let's try something with our clothes on for a few hours. If I need to go get changed, I will."

His gaze landed on my leggings, which were sprinkled with words like boom, kapow, and bang. I'd paired them with a long, fluffy white sweater. My fancy outfit.

"No, you're dressed perfectly for my idea."

When he parked outside of a huge warehouse-style building, I read the sign and couldn't possibly connect it with a date night. Other than it might be the best date night *ever*.

An indoor trampoline park.

He killed the engine and I knew he wasn't joking. He turned toward me, light from the parking lot glinting off his impeccable hair and shadowing his blue eyes.

"I have a pair of sweats in my overnight bag." He reached into the backseat to dig them out, wearing a half-smile, like his excitement was growing as much as mine.

"I've always wanted to go here but I never had anyone to go with."

He paused briefly. "What about that good friend of yours?"

I laughed. "Sam? He would've loved it, but I think by the time I met him, he wasn't in shape anymore. From the way he talked, it would've been something he and his son would've loved back in the day. Too bad…"

Whoa. I'd almost said too much. Sam Robson had passed, but it wasn't my place to spread his personal business.

My Sam was waiting for me to finish my thought. "Too bad what?"

I opened my mouth to speak but stalled at the bleakness in his gaze. My heart sank. Sam had lost his father, too.

"Nothing. I just wish he could've healed his relationship with his son. I guess he passed on the business know-how, but personally, he'd felt those bridges were burned."

"Why would he? What would make a father feel that?" Wes's tone was neutral, but his brow was creased as if he couldn't understand it. Neither could I.

I shrugged, growing uncomfortable with the topic. "He said after the divorce that his ex sent the boy away for school. Then he was gone for college. After that, well, he had no one to hand the reins of the company to, so that's all their relationship became."

His eye twitched. "I don't think that'd stop a real dad from seeing his kid."

"Perhaps he didn't think he was a real dad." That was the closest I would come to airing my dear friend's business. Maybe one day, when I trusted the man next to me completely, I could talk about how awful I'd felt for my friend and, at one time, his son.

Sam shook his head, not understanding, but before he said anything, I waved it off.

"I know, I didn't agree with it, either, but he was from a different time, and honestly, those with money just think differently from us."

He opened his mouth to say something but closed it and passed me a small smile. "I heard they have an obstacle course here and I think I can totally beat you."

"Oh, you're on."

CHAPTER 12

ara

I WOKE up before my alarm. Another Saturday, another game day. We were winding down.

Sam slumbered next to me. I studied his features, glad to see his lines of stress from the previous week gone.

Geez, he was a gorgeous man. Strong jaw, straight nose, healthy glow that showed he wasn't imprisoned in an office all day. My gaze drifted down to his muscular shoulders and defined chest.

I could fall hard for him. Because of how considerate he'd been the weekend before with my mother. And how he'd good-naturedly worn a costume, then after we'd eaten out, I'd sworn he would've taken Mom out dancing had I said the word.

Then last night. I hadn't laughed that much with a guy, or gotten so sweaty with one with my clothes on.

Swinging my legs down, I arched my back in a stretch. Oh

yeah, I was going to be stiff today. Worth every protesting muscle to have that kind of fun with Sam.

My mouth quirked. Sam. I'd lost a dear friend, only to find someone who could become very special to me with the same name. Was the big guy reaching down from above, still trying to find a way to help me out?

The year of therapy after my college nightmare had been priceless. Otherwise, I'd have never let men like Sam Robson, Chris, and Ephraim into my life. I'd learned to balance my personal desperation with solid decision-making—after protecting myself first, of course. Maybe one day I'd deeply trust a man.

A hand snaked out and wrapped around my waist to pull me back into bed.

"Hey." I laughed and cuddled into him. "I have to get to work."

"It's Saturday," he mumbled into my hair.

"Game day in my world, and one of the last ones."

His grip loosened.

Well, wasn't my morning bittersweet. I only had a few more gaming Saturdays to enjoy, but it meant I had to leave a morning in bed with Sam.

"Stay as long as you want, I know it's early. I gotta shower."

I showered, but before I could shut the water off, the door opened.

Turned out shower sex started the morning out right.

I was still grinning as I opened up the store. Sam had even asked if he could stop by later.

The day got started as normal. Joe and Ephraim for another round of Axis & Allies. Chris even jumped into the fray.

The time went by quickly, but every time the door dinged, I looked up with a surge of hope.

Maybe Sam had work. Or had a family. He rarely talked about his family. Just him and his mom and he made her sound like a hot mess.

"We'll clean up," Ephraim called across the room, "and get out of your hair."

"No rush. I have no plans tonight." Dating Sam was spoiling her. Nights with nothing going on didn't offer the appeal they used to.

My door's bell dinged and I spun with a smile to greet my next customer.

Sam walked in, eyeing the interior of my store cautiously like he didn't know what to expect.

I shoved my hands into the back pockets of my favorite jeans and sauntered over to him.

The corner of his mouth quirked and he strolled to meet me.

He must've run home to change because he was wearing athletic pants and a maroon University of Chicago sweatshirt.

"You made it." I rose to my tiptoes to greet him with a kiss.

He draped an arm around my shoulders and we wandered through my store. "Absolutely. I couldn't ask you what you were doing tonight, otherwise." A gaming system on the wall caught his attention. "Is this for real?"

He broke away and picked up the gray PlayStation.

"Chris got his hands on one of the first models. It doesn't work, unfortunately, but it's a nice decoration. And I'm sure he secretly thinks he can fix it."

"I remember getting one of these when they first came out. Sa— My dad and I would play all night. And since I was like, seven, it'd piss my mom off so much."

I chuckled and noticed Joe staring at us. Ephraim was

glancing up occasionally, but his expression was more curious where Joe's looked stunned.

Sam had that effect on people.

"Let me introduce you to two of my friends." I grabbed his hand and pulled him along. "Joe, Ephraim, this is Sam. He's a fanboy in disguise."

Sam smiled and reached his hand out.

"How ya doing, Sam?" Ephraim pumped Sam's hand and went back to picking up the tiny pieces of the game.

"Joe," Sam greeted.

Joe nodded but said nothing. He turned his back on us to help Ephraim, which surprised me. Joe was a little quieter than many customers but always sociable.

"So, Sam," Ephraim said. "It's too bad you won't be able to join us for many more game days."

"I heard. I'm not much of a board gamer. I need graphics and a console."

They both chuckled. Sam asked about Axis & Allies and after Ephraim filled him in, Sam stepped away and pulled me with him.

"Nice to meet you two." When we were near the cash register, he leaned down to my ear. "So, are you free tonight?"

"I might be. What do you have in mind?"

"I think we could fire up that Xbox of yours. I have a competition in mind that involves someone getting naked."

A thrill shot through me. I'd been thoroughly sexed the night before, but with Sam, it didn't matter. "You're on. Swing by around seven-thirty and I'll even feed you."

The kiss he gave me before he left was full of promise. With a sigh, I flipped my closed sign over and turned to Ephraim and Joe.

Ephraim hefted the game box under his arm but stopped with a concerned look at Joe. "You all right, man?"

Joe cleared his throat and spoke to Mara. "What'd you say his name was?"

I tilted my head at him, unsure of his concerned expression. "Sam."

Joe's gaze went to the door, then back to me. His face had lost some color. "Mara...that's Wesley Robson."

"Joe!" A nervous chuckle burst out of me. "What are you talking about?"

"Joe?" Ephraim echoed.

"That man was Wes Robson. I see him almost every day I work. Apparently, he doesn't see me." Joe shrugged and looked down at his outfit of jeans and a T-shirt. "I'm usually in coveralls, I guess."

I stared at Joe and the world quit spinning. I blocked out everything but Joe's news.

No. It couldn't be. My Sam was *not* Wes. A lump lodged square in my chest.

Ephraim set the game down and straightened. "Where did you meet him again?"

I swallowed because I hated the answer. "At Canon, Wes Robson's nightclub." I pulled out a chair and collapsed in it. "I asked for him at the bar and low and behold, this guy sat next to me and struck up a conversation."

It had to be a coincidence. Sam only resembled Wes Robson. And was in his club...with the same name as Wes Robson's dad... Disbelief rocked my being.

"And he told you his name was Sam?" Ephraim's voice was gentle.

Pushing my bangs out of my face, I kept my hands on my head. How could I be... "I'm so stupid."

"Mara," Joe shuffled closer, "it's not your fault."

I peered up at him. Maybe Joe was mistaken. He only passed his boss every day, it's not like they were close. "Are you sure?"

Joe gave me a sad nod.

"Let's pull up his picture." Ephraim took the seat next to me to search on his phone.

My laugh was harsh and bitter. "I was going to do the same thing when Sam—ugh, Wes—started hitting on me."

Tears burned the back of my eyes, but I refused to cry until I was alone. Ephraim spun his phone toward me. On the screen was a stolid picture of Sam—Wes— in a suit and tie, a headshot that was used for his profile on his website.

"That's him." My heart crumbled, cut under the knife of betrayal. Well, didn't I feel foolish. Like the stupidest, most naïve girl on earth. I'd let my guard down and *wham!* Stupid girl. "Why would he do that?"

"My guess is daddy issues. He wants to know why his dad was going to basically give this place to you."

I scoffed. "I bet he assumed I slept my way into that contract. Of course, that's what anyone would think." My cheeks flamed. These men were my customers and they'd just witnessed a humiliation that blew Dr. Johannsen out of this realm. At least I was the only one hurt this time.

Joe shook his head with disgust and laid a hand on my shoulder. "He grew up differently than us. In his world, relationships are a contract in and of themselves."

I scrubbed my face. "What do I do?"

Ephraim swore and pocketed his phone. "Would you like me to come with you when you confront him?"

Joe bobbed his head. "I'll even go with you, Mara. He can't get away with what he's done."

Confront Wes in front of an audience? Absolutely not. Humiliation, party of one. "No. You're not putting your job on the line." Betrayal gave way to anger. "No, you know what? I'm not confronting him. He wants to play some secretive game and dig for information, I can, too."

"Mara…" Ephraim's look was one I'd expect from a father

who was afraid his little girl would get hurt. Ironically, it was one I'd gotten from Sam—the real Sam—when we'd talked business and he'd feared for my financial state.

"I know. But I need to know why he'd do this to me and he won't tell me if I out him."

Joe cut in. "Mr. Robson isn't known for relationships. There are rumors of course, but nothing serious, and he never brings it to the office. I'm surprised he's even making an effort." Joe's kind smile was another I would've loved from a father. "He might not even know why he's doing what he's doing."

Joe might be trying to make me feel better, but Wes's behavior was inexcusable. My falling for it was just as bad.

Ephraim cleared his throat. His elbows were propped on his thighs, his hands pressed together at the fingertips between his knees. His serious expression was all lawyer. "As much as I'd like to think he has legitimately fallen for you because you're a good person, and he'd be an idiot not to, Wesley Robson is not a stupid person. He inherited everything, but he was a force in his own right before his dad passed away. He knows full well that he can't deceive you forever, but he's continuing to. You have to wonder why."

"He even asked me out tonight," I muttered miserably. For all my talk of playing the same game, facing him after work sunk a boulder in my gut. My courage was nothing more than words.

The urge to crawl out of my skin grew stronger. I rose and gave each guy a quick hug. Because what the hell, my store was closing and they were my friends. If Wes Robson could do something as slimy as lying his way into my bed, then he wasn't going to have mercy on my store.

"Thank you, guys. I mean it. I'm going to go along with it, for now." Because I didn't know what else to do. The idea of Sam wasn't one my heart wanted to let go of.

Imagine that. Another handsome man was using me for selfish purposes. At least Wes wasn't married. His duplicity only hurt me.

"Be safe, Mara. I don't think he'll hurt you, but…"

I squeezed Ephraim's hand. No, I didn't think Wes would lay a hand on me. He had all the power anyway. He couldn't hurt me any more than he already had.

∼

Wes

"Wesley, I think I'm dying."

"You're not dying, Mother." I sat on Mara's front step. It was a little after seven-thirty and she was late.

"It's the cold. It's going to do me in. Have you rented that villa in the islands for me yet?"

"I'm not renting a villa." But it was tempting. Months of my mom out of the state. Out of the country. What held me back was the tab she'd rack up because I'd have to open a line of credit for her to use.

"It's either the villa or a hospital bill. I'm telling you, I won't survive another Minnesota winter. Perhaps I'll need to move in with you."

"Stay inside and order in. They deliver everything nowadays. And no, you can't live with me." Access to my housekeeper, chef, and driver was what she really wanted. She coveted my private jet, too.

"We'll talk about this later. I have another doctor's visit and he'll write a note. Not that I should need one for my own son," she finished with sarcasm.

It wouldn't matter, but I let my mom hang up. Villa or a

hospital bill. I toed a rock off the step. Would I even visit once or twice a week like Mara did with her mother?

Mara could visit my mother, too. They could both worm their way into my bank accounts. Even the thought was half-hearted because, despite my best efforts, Mara wasn't giving me those vibes.

I breathed a sigh of relief when she finally pulled up. How'd that girl always pull me out of my head?

I went to go open her car door, but I stalled at the look on her face. Stricken. My bubbly girl looked like she faced her worst nightmare.

I pulled open the door and held out my hand. "You okay?"

She pursed her delectable lips and shoved two fast food bags into my hands. "It just hit me today. Some asshole's closing my store out of spite and I can do nothing about it." She got out and charged toward her front door. "Sorry, I didn't feel like cooking."

The door banged back on me as I followed her. Kicking it open, I stepped in and peeked in the bag.

"Burgers are fine." I usually ate clean but a night of fries, whose grease had already soaked through the bag, wouldn't clog my arteries in one shot. Maybe.

I doled out the food at her small table.

"I left a perky woman at the store a couple of hours ago and she came here pissed as hell. What happened?"

She considered me for so long I shifted in my seat, didn't dare bite into my sandwich. Strong feelings simmered in the depths of her hazel beauties and it was disconcerting to feel like it was aimed at me.

"Sam, why are you here?"

"Because we made a date."

She stabbed a fry into ketchup and popped it into her mouth. I did the same.

"It's just that," she continued after she swallowed, "you seem like a successful guy. You're hot and you know it. I'm going out of business, I dress in clothes covered in superheroes, and my history with men is... Well, I haven't made the best decisions."

"So, you're wondering what I see in you?" Did she hear the incredulous tone in my voice? I hoped so. Yeah, I was in this for other reasons. But say she hadn't conned my dad—she was *smokin'*. And ambitious. And sweet and funny and—argh. Was I going to prove Flynn right and quote Shakespeare next?

My voice dropped low. "Do I need to show you again?"

Her eyes narrowed on me. "Maybe later."

We ate in silence. My chef would go apoplectic if he saw what I had just ingested. This entire meal probably wouldn't buy the one-serving side dish Chef prepared for me at each meal.

"I haven't played *Halo* in forever and I noticed you have the game. Gonna let me warm up before you take me on?"

"Nope." She dumped our garbage and went to the living room.

We set up on the floor, backs against the couch, end table pushed out of the way. I was half-hard already, remembering what we'd done on that couch. My personal vendetta to reveal her greedy nature was going to have to wait. My temporary mission was to cheer her up, not because it bothered me that much—it didn't—but because I wanted access to her body and Mara was as closed off as my office.

I got a few giggles out of her. Especially when I died horrible deaths in the game.

"All right, enough of *Halo*. What else do you have?"

"I'll get one more your speed." She crawled to the console and switched out games, giving me a prime view of her ass.

I adjusted myself, but it was no use.

When she came back, I pulled her onto my lap. She tensed instead of melting into me like usual.

I captured her mouth in a kiss, but her wooden response wasn't promising.

"Mara, what's wrong?" I brushed her bangs out of her eyes.

"I...I just don't know anymore." Her eyes glistened. "I'm so tired of everything."

"Let me help you forget about it tonight."

Her placid stare remained in place.

Okay. "Then how 'bout you use me as your personal stress reliever?" I released my hold on her and leaned back against the couch. "Use me."

She waited so long, I'd taken sex off the table for the night. Then she straddled me and jerked my sweater up. I helped her remove it and shuffled my pants down. Before I tossed them, I grabbed a condom out of my pocket.

I fisted the hem of her shirt, but she pushed my hands away to stand. Mara peeling her jeans down was an erotic show I'd pay thousands to watch. When she was bared to me, I fisted myself and gave my cock a sturdy stroke. I was as physically excited as I was mentally with Mara using me for her purposes.

She knelt back in front of me, that damn shirt still on, her nipples poking through the fabric. I licked my lips but held back from tonguing them through the cloth. This was her show.

She ripped open the packet and rolled it on me.

"Do you need to be prepped?" I slid my hand along her thigh, my gaze buried in the view of her mounting me.

To answer, she lifted and settled herself over me to slide down.

I groaned but registered that she had misled me. She wasn't as wet as usual, but the condom lubricated her entrance enough for me to slide in. I went to grab her hips, but she flung my hands off.

I anchored them on the edges of the cushions. She hoisted herself up and slammed down. My breath whooshed out.

"Fuck, Mara." I had to spread my legs a little, with a slight bend at the knees. My fingers dug into threadbare upholstery.

She rose and came down hard again. Her hands gripped my shoulders. Written across her face was determination. To get off? She oughta know I'd never let her down in that arena.

She rode me hard. I grunted at the force of holding my orgasm back until she went.

Her lower lip was sucked in and captured by her teeth. I wanted to be the one nibbling on it, but for some alien reason, I had to let her use me. I'd give her what she needed. For once, my pleasure wasn't the goal.

She let out a little cry and her head flung back. Her neck was exposed and her eyes were closed.

"Look at me, Mara." Who knew why it was so important, but it was. She needed to know who she was with. That was it. The connection.

Her pace increased, she grew wetter, easing the blow to my ego.

"I can't—" she panted. "This is—" Her lids shut and her fingernails dug in as her climax hit.

Her mouth dropped open and I waited for her to yell Sam but it never came. She hollered her orgasm and I gritted my teeth against mine.

The episode affected me. First, the unusual way she'd acted tonight, then the frantic ride. I wrapped her up in an embrace and spun her to the floor with me on top.

Her eyes flew open with a gasp, but I'd already claimed her mouth.

Murmuring against her lips, I said, "Now it's my turn."

I pumped and she responded, sluggishly at first, probably due to her recent orgasm and the change of position.

I broke away from our kiss to hitch her legs up. She'd used me and I'd told her to, but my male side needed to dominate.

Her hands dropped back behind her head. That shirt. I growled and yanked it up to expose her breasts. The bra was in the way, but not for long. Freeing her breasts, I gave in and lapped at one nipple, then the other.

Mara moaned and writhed under me. I couldn't hold back a smug smile. She was unable to control herself and I made sure of it.

Her walls started to quake around me and I finally broke down the dam holding back my orgasm. Slamming once, twice more, my balls tightened and I thrust one last time before bowing back.

"Mara!" My buttocks tightened and I shook my release into her.

Like before, her orgasm was on the quiet side. She didn't yell my name like she normally did, and if I were honest, it was a relief not to hear the wrong name while the girl I fucked came all over me.

Her lids were half open and she lazily watched me, but there was a hint of caution in the depths of her gaze. She was usually so open with her feelings, I hated closed-off Mara.

I released her legs and they collapsed to the floor.

"You gonna tell me what's wrong yet?"

She tilted her head and the halo of pink-dyed hair shifted, too. "What makes you think there's something wrong?"

Her tone also asked, *why do you care?* And I didn't. I cursed to myself. Then why did I keep asking?

She was spread out under me, not completely naked, but all her beautiful anatomy was revealed.

I kissed each breast and she tensed like she was going to get up, but I continued kissing my way down.

Again, she didn't say anything but widened her legs to allow me room to bury my face in her well-sexed flesh. Another orgasm might get her talking.

CHAPTER 13

ara

I STARED AT THE CEILING, having woken up first. Sam had stayed over.

I squeezed my eyes shut. *Wes*. Would I ever get used to it? Wes Robson was in my bed. One thing was for sure. I could fantasize laughing in his receptionist's face. He could've been in all the meetings in the world, but I'd still been able to talk to him after all. With no clothes on.

I turned to the slumbering man.

Wesley Robson. In my bed.

Was this like sleeping with the enemy?

I'd known who he was last night and I'd gone along with it. I felt dirty and guilty, and guilty for not feeling dirty because I didn't. Sex with Wes was too wonderful to feel ashamed for seeking my release with him.

With my history, I should be in the tub, scrubbing his taste out of my mouth. But he wasn't Dr. Johannsen, either.

My esteemed professor had been attractive enough, but not the male specimen Wes was. Nor as good in bed.

Not that I'd wanted to be in bed with my professor, but the man had been smart and I'd been gullible and desperate.

I think I can see a way to help you improve your grade.

Stupid.

And this wasn't?

I peered at Wes again. No, because I knew what I was doing this time. My eyes were wide open.

He adjusted his position and reached for me. There went my damn heart. He wasn't able to fake fooling me in his sleep.

His dark hair was mussed and not just from being in bed. When I'd first seen him, I'd compared him to a superhero. How disappointing.

Joe mentioned people like Wes didn't always have healthy relationships.

I frowned and skimmed my fingers across his cheek. Was I really going to analyze him, after all his deception? Yeah, I was. He'd said his dad had passed away and I of all people had heard from the real Sam all of his regrets about how he had treated Wes. Then there was Wes's mom. Geez, she'd sounded unreal. Like a cartoon stereotype of the wicked ex-wife. And she'd raised Wes.

I turned fully on my side to face him. What if I didn't play him in return, but tried to show him the other side of life? Real relationships that weren't driven by greed? My relationship with my mom was real. My friendship with Sam had been legit, and nothing more than platonic. Ephraim and Joe had families to go home to, but Sam hadn't had anyone. Feeling like he'd lost Wes, he had thrown his love into the comic book shop. To keep those memories alive.

Wes's eyelids fluttered before those startling blues met

mine. His lips tilted in a sleepy smile as he rolled onto his back to stretch.

"I usually visit my mom on Sundays."

He smirked at me. "You're kicking me out."

I rolled up to prop myself on an elbow. "Or...you could come with?"

"Sure. It'd be great to hang with Wendy again. Is this what was bothering you last night? Did you think your mom would scare me off?"

What a fabulous excuse. "Kind of. I like you." *Before I found out you were a disingenuous man who was out for what—a revenge fuck?*

Greatest sex of my life. Got me good, asshole.

"Of course I don't mind. It's refreshing to be around a mom who... acts like a mom."

I tried to keep the pity out of my look. "Really?"

His lopsided smile softened my heart. "Was it a ploy to get me to go away?"

"No. It was a real invite. I have one other question. Do you play rummy?"

Wes

I WAS on my third hand of rummy.

It was fun.

Mara's mom was just as pleasant as before and had been delighted when I'd walked in. What would it be like to grow up with a mom like that?

"Wendy, I do believe you've won this round again."

Wendy chuckled, her brown eyes lighting up. I didn't

think I could say anything wrong around her. I just enjoyed the conversation.

How would my mom behave around Mara?

Easy—atrociously. My mom would demean and condescend, and nitpick Mara's appearance and weight. All before she found out about Mara's relationship with Sam. Then no holds barred, get your gloves out, fight club only has one rule.

Mara gathered the cards and shuffled them. "Do you need me to bring anything on Tuesday when I swing by?"

"Whenever you have time to make a library run, I'd appreciate it. More audiobooks, please. Cards are easier to hold, but books can wear my hands out."

"Sure. I'll grab some tonight and bring 'em." Mara packed up our stuff and we stood to leave.

"Thank you." Wendy smiled at me and waved. "Nice to see you again, Sam."

"I never pass up the chance to visit a lady who can whip me at cards."

She giggled and it took twenty years off her tired features.

When I turned, I was struck by Mara's look of awe.

I nudged her with an elbow as we walked through the narrow corridors. "You're looking all shocked that I can charm your mother."

"I expected you to be a little uncomfortable with, you know, the environment. Comic-Con's a little different than hanging out in a nursing home."

I shrugged. It was surprisingly homey in the place.

Mara grabbed my hand. "Do you mind stopping at the library with me? They don't close for a couple of hours."

"If I get lost, will you find me?"

She chuckled, but I wasn't joking. I'd never been in a public library.

CHAPTER 14

ara

I KISSED Wes at the door as I was leaving for work Monday morning. He'd stayed over again and another supreme night of amazing sex had firmed my resolve to show him that I was a decent person.

"When do I get to see your place?"

His brows rose in surprise. "Uh…my place isn't the best for entertaining."

I swept my arm around my living room. "And my humble abode is magnificent?"

"It's homier than mine." Probably not a lie. "My place is large and obnoxious. I don't know why I bought it."

"Condo?"

"House."

Oh. A mansion. Did he have staff? Would they see me and wonder why he'd ever bring a girl like me around?

"I'd better get to work. Lock up when you leave?"

"Always." He clasped my wrist as I stepped away. "Wednesday night?"

"I don't know. Are you going to keep me up all night again?"

"Probably."

My body celebrated. Geez, I should feel guilty. But the sex. My body craved it more the longer we were together like he was an addiction.

I went through the day in a daze of sorting, marking down the last of my stock for clearance, and explaining the situation to customers who hadn't yet heard. After a busier weekend than normal and the added stress of Wes, I was lagging by the end of the day.

The sign was turned to officially closed when Chris spoke up. "I talked to my friend. She's been looking into it, double-checking all the permits are filed correctly. Wes Robson hasn't been her favorite person since he made them jump through hoops to expedite the approval process for the outlet mall, then switched his plans to St. Paul."

"It won't be in time to stop the store from closing. He owns the building."

"But like you said, we can be a burr in his backside. Guys like him don't understand what they do to us when they swing their power and money around."

The Wes who'd been so considerate and charming with my mother contradicted the man who was shutting me down.

"I don't know. I feel like I should just drop it." I hadn't told Chris my new man was really Wes.

Chris punched into the register to count the money. "It's out of our hands now. It's not you if that makes you feel better. My friend got an ulcer from the stress he put her through. The whole office hates him. Except for the young women."

"Thank you for thinking of the store." Wes seemed so untouchable, I doubted Chris's contact would have any luck.

My phone rang. "Hey, Ephraim."

"Mara, can you swing by the office so we can get your signatures on some papers?"

Spend Friday through Sunday with Wes, launch legal action against him by Monday. Who had I turned into? I knew who he was, I shouldn't play along, and I wasn't *that* person. I wasn't him. But…he shouldn't get away with it. He didn't get to play with my emotions, string me along, all the while knowing he was responsible for shutting down my dream and driving me into a financial corner. My resolve was strengthened. I'd pretend ignorance and date "Sam."

My store closed later than regular businesses, so traffic wasn't bad on the way to Ephraim's firm.

He was the only one there, to my relief. We went through and I signed and initialed and got my own stack of copies.

Ephraim walked me to the door. "What did you decide?"

He'd waited until the end, I was glad.

"I'm trying to show him I'm a decent person and that maybe he is, too."

His expression turned wary. "People like Wes won't look at it that way. When he finds out, and he will find out, Mara, he'll attach to the fact that you knew. That's all he'll care about. You knew who he really was and you didn't say anything."

"I have a little faith in him."

Ephraim's paternal expression was full of warning. It was becoming a standard look for him. "Even after you signed papers to look into the contract Sam had Robson Industries draw up?"

"It's buying us time." I stifled a groan. Just like Chris's friend was trying to do.

This was messed up.

"Tread carefully, Mara. He has the money to make life difficult for you."

"He has money—he's not a mobster."

"Sometimes there's a fine line."

I didn't know rich people. Ephraim saw the worst of them. Should I drop everything and tell Wes I know about his game?

Climbing back into my car and settling inside, I resisted hitting my head against the steering wheel.

I should be angry at Wes for not meeting with me in the first place. If he had, this would have been avoided. All of it, including our relationship. But he was as stubborn as his father.

And I should've done more research. But his office was across the street from my store so I hadn't bothered to look up anything about him, or even see what he looked like. Still didn't justify what he was doing.

My phone pinged with a text. From Wes.

Missing you.

My heart twisted. Sweet or calculating? Miss you, too.

Bed's pretty empty w/o u.

So's my floor.

And the counter. Night.

What a mess. His messages made me feel better that I was going home to an empty house and he was in an empty bed.

Wes

IT WAS the middle of the week and I was going through Mara withdrawals. Pathetic. We'd been sending sweet texts back and forth, something completely out of my realm.

I brought my attention back to Helen, who was giving me midweek updates.

"I have some unsettling news." She knew better than to pause. "The city council's office called and they said we need to resubmit for all required demolition permits."

"What the hell for? I thought it was all taken care of."

"A glitch."

"A glitch?"

"Yes sir. I smell a sewer at full capacity."

"And if we argue about this glitch?" We'd done everything by the book. I always did. No corner-cutting, no favors called in. I might push the boundaries and be demanding, but I *followed the rules*.

"I argued up main street and down the highway. Even talked to the head of the department. She was less than willing to cooperate."

She would be. Still raw from me moving my outlet mall plans across the river.

"It'll delay the project more than initially anticipated," Helen answered, "and add a little more expense. That should be the worst of it."

Why now? Everything had been coasting along. The outdated mall was closing its doors in less than three weeks.

Chris offered to contact an old friend on the city commission.

I clenched my jaw. So, that's how she wanted to play it. First, the lawsuit that my legal team was in a catfight over, and now this.

She wanted to be a PITA? She thought she was smarter than my dad and now she thought she could undermine me, using the men around her to do her bidding. What else were the men around her doing for her? "Helen, write this name down. Mara Jade Baranski. I want to know everything about her."

Helen scribbled her name. "Arcadia's owner? What should I be searching for?"

"Anything that points to her character. She's the one behind this delay. Trust me."

"She's grasping at straws. First taking legal action against Robson Industries, and now this." Helen shook her head. "Some people can't make an honest living."

Note to self: give Helen a raise.

After work, I strode out to my car. Instead of picking her up for dinner, I'd left a message that there was a change of plans—due to a *glitch* in the reservation. My chef had prepped dinner for two, one that wouldn't set up shop in my arteries, and delivered it to my office so I could take it over to Mara's.

We were going to eat in and I was going to relieve my stress in her body. Many times.

CHAPTER 15

ara

I FINISHED INVENTORY. Stock was moving at a good rate. The second to last game day was tomorrow and I'd mark the used Xboxes for sale.

"Got any fun Friday plans that'd put mine to shame?" Chris called from the front where he was closing up.

"I have a date." If it turned out like Wednesday night's, should I be thrilled or dismayed?

I'd been looking forward to real food and not something out of a can when Wes had canceled dinner out. Instead, he'd brought over an excellent meal, and I'd barely had any time to enjoy it before he had been stripping me down.

All night long, he'd been at me. When he'd been too spent, he'd used his tongue or his fingers. I'd physically pushed him off my bed and demanded a few hours' sleep before work on Thursday.

He'd given it to me, only to wake me up before my alarm for another round.

Not a bad way to wake up, but I was convinced that death by orgasm was real.

Chris locked up and handed me the envelope of money to deposit. "Hey, did I tell you I heard back from my friend? She wants to thank you. Wes was so pissed at the delays and she found it refreshing that their roles were reversed."

I laid the envelope on her desk and scowled at it. "When was this?"

"Wednesday, I think."

Uh-huh. "That's good then?"

"Yeah, it won't stop anything, but it's worth it, right?"

Tell her vagina that.

No, don't. It might agree.

"See you tomorrow?"

I nodded woodenly and sank into my seat. So the sex wasn't because he found me irresistible. He'd been upset at me and had used me all night long.

Anger burned through me. My cheeks grew hot and my breathing rate kicked up. How could he? I'd thought that despite the deceit we'd connected, whether he wanted to admit it to himself or not. Had I fooled myself yet again? Looking at the time, I groaned. I had an hour to pull myself together and calm down before meeting him.

Wes

I WAITED in front of the restaurant where Mara had been adamant about meeting me. Was she getting weird on me again?

I'd been…intense…the other night, but most women would come begging for more.

As Mara walked up with a stoop in her shoulders, wearing those ridiculous Batman leggings I loved, she didn't have a begging mood about her.

"There she is," I greeted.

I got a half-smile. Yep, she was stuck in her head.

"Sorry, I'm not feeling too well tonight," she said in a soft voice.

"I heard they have good food here. Eat a solid meal and you'll feel better."

I held the door open for her and she muttered something as she walked by.

"What was that?"

"Nothing."

We were seated and she folded and unfolded her napkin while staring out the window.

"Mara?"

"Everything with my store," she blurted. "It's just— How could he treat me like that?"

Her eyes shimmered, and as a sign of how much I'd emotionally opened up to her, I sought to comfort her instead of putting as much distance between us as possible. I could barely believe what I was doing as I reached a hand across the table, but she stared at it.

"What if I have to dig into my reserves and I run out of money to pay for my mom's care?"

Her words tugged on my conscience, but I pushed it aside rather than owning it. Wendy needed to be in a nursing home. But where had Mara's reserves come from? Helen would find out. Besides, Mara was smart, she could get a decent job easy. A regular nine-to-fiver with good benefits.

She dabbed at her eyes. "I'm sorry. I'm not going to be good company tonight."

"You can't scare me away."

The words were meant to soothe, but instead, she wiped tears away.

All through dinner, I made inane small talk while her glassy stare unraveled my heart. For the hundredth time, I questioned what I was doing with Mara, how it was all going to end, for me and for her—for us. I followed her back to her place and we watched a movie. Nothing physical beyond me holding her.

It was early when we'd usually be seeing way beyond midnight together, but I tucked us into her bed.

Grudgingly, I had to admit it was my best night of sleep ever. I would've slept in, but her alarm went off.

Game day. She rolled out of bed without a backward glance and padded to the bathroom to shower.

She'd be working all day, and I'd…work? I was behind with Canon's paperwork but nothing critical. A Saturday morning at the club was ideal for being productive. I wasn't meeting with Franklin about my plans in New York until later in the week.

I reclined on her bed and watched her dress and get ready for work.

"Lock up when you leave?" she asked.

"Aren't you going to have breakfast?"

"Chris is bringing donuts today and probably for our last game day next week."

"What if I'm still here when you get home?"

She was walking out of the bedroom and glanced back in surprise. "What if I'm not feeling any better?"

"Then I'll take care of you again." And I meant it. Why? The time was coming when I had to cease being Sam. I'd go back to being the…what? The guy who worked all the time? The successful businessman who women flocked to? Would I take my pick and be okay not knowing a thing about my partner and knowing our interaction was barely more than a verbal contract?

An unreadable expression flitted over her face, but she settled back on neutral. "I should probably get some groceries."

Morbidly interested in how she chose what canned or boxed goodness to buy, I said, "Come back first and I'll go with you."

She nodded and left.

The silence of her house bothered me, unlike mine. I rarely used the main floor of my house, keeping to the upper level I'd made my lair. The weekends when I had no staff around, I didn't mind the quiet.

In Mara's place, I did.

What to do all day. I could be a slug and game the hours away. Stopping in the bathroom, my gaze kept going to the drippy faucet. Mara's shower hadn't yet drained in the tub.

In the kitchen, I couldn't escape the steady drip from that sink, either. Might as well unplug her fridge for all the food it contained. Leaving to get something for breakfast was the first order of business.

I pulled aside the drapes to check the weather outside. One end of her picture window was missing a screen and I didn't have to look out the window to guess the temperature because the cold air drafted through the frame.

Locating my phone, I called Flynn. My buddy owned an industrial construction company and was just who I needed.

"Grab your tools and something to eat and get over here. I'll text you the address."

My groggy friend mumbled a curse and I heard a female's voice reply.

We hung up and I texted Flynn directions to Mara's.

Flynn's reply: U owe me. Morning wood doesn't take care of itself.

I dressed and had time to play a few rounds of *Super Mario* before Flynn knocked on the door.

"What a freaking dive, dude."

Defensive instinct rose. "It's not that bad."

Flynn snorted and came inside. He carried a bag of food in one hand and an old, dusty bag of tools in the other.

"How long has it been since you've gotten your hands dirty?" I asked.

"Fuck you. I still do some work. Usually on the weekends so I don't have to put up with anyone." Flynn set his bag down but didn't come any farther inside. "Besides. I like to see how the contractors dick with me when they think I don't know what they're talking about."

I grabbed the food. "I'm starving. You should see what that girl eats."

"If it looks like this place, I don't want to." Finally moving inside, he didn't stop, roaming Mara's house. "Ready to get your hands dirty, bro?"

Yeah, actually, I was. I looked forward to hanging out with Flynn and improving Mara's home.

CHAPTER 16

ara

I DIDN'T WANT to face Wes. Not after the paradox of last night. The way he'd taken care of me and tucked me in.

Could I be getting through to him or was it still some elaborate ruse to prove…what? Whatever reason had made him introduce himself as Sam was no longer the reason he stayed Sam. I doubted he'd ever watched a movie with a girl and not gotten past first base. The naïve girl inside of me I couldn't get away from suggested the intimacy we shared was more than just sex. We enjoyed each other's company, were physically compatible, and had similar interests. How many couples could watch season after season of Star Trek together? That was more than sex.

Yet I was the one who was ultimately behind his troubles with the city, and how could I forget the lawsuit?

Useless. All of it. While he may be deceiving me, I'd had

no reason to think he did dirty business. Even Chris's friend had had to make up a reason to stall Wes's plans.

But I'd go along with it because it might buy some time for Wes to come around. Dare I wish for him to apologize for how he'd acted? It was the best-case scenario. The opposite outcome could get very ugly.

It was already dark when I pulled up to my house. Wes jogged outside to meet me and climbed in.

Instantly my mood lifted with his ready grin. Then the deep kiss he gave me wiped out the rest of my melancholy.

What was between us was *real*. Had to be.

"Where to?" he murmured against my mouth. "Or should we sit here for a while and keep each other warm?"

"Groceries first. And then you can warm me up."

I backed out while he buckled up. As I drove to the store, I wondered if Wes had ever been in one. Was grocery shopping too plebian of a task? Did he have "people" who did these kinds of things?

My question was answered as Wes darted from stand to stand. He stopped to read greeting cards and trotted over to show me the funny ones. "People still send these?"

Then he picked up everything I tossed in the cart and read the ingredients.

"There's not even real cheese in this."

"No," I agreed. "But a box of mac and cheese costs a dollar and a small brick of cheese costs four."

He grabbed canned green beans. "Look at the sodium in this."

"I drain and rinse them first. It helps."

He wandered next to me, more subdued. "But even frozen has to be better."

"While I could eat healthier on a budget, I'm sticking to dirt cheap until I get back on my feet after Arcadia closes."

I watched him closely. He scowled and a zing of satisfaction went through me. He had no idea how the rest of us lived. Never wondered where his next paycheck was coming from. Never been run out of business by a resentful real estate tycoon.

What must it be like for him? See it, buy it. No thought of cost. No waffling between canned and frozen, or eating based on the weekly sale ad. A million dollars could land in my lap and I didn't think my thrifty tendencies would vanish.

We waited to check out and while I noticed all the appreciative glances he received, he inspected the magazines.

"Have you heard of this new movie with the Greek gods?"

I nodded and smiled fondly. "I never read the books but I'm going to the movie. Anything Greek has a fond place in my heart."

I began unloading my items on the belt and Wes stepped in to help.

"I was thinking that after this, I wanted to make one stop," I said.

"Whatever. You're driving." He dropped his head to whisper, "I'm at your mercy."

He might not be after I played the last card I had left against Wes's power and money.

I explained my reasons without telling him where we were going. "I really appreciate you doing this with me. It's just that I've not gotten the chance to visit this place for months. I should have this summer, but with Arcadia closing, I just feel like I need to stop and pay my respects."

Out of the corner of my eyes, Wes's expression froze. Inch by inch, he turned to face me.

"Where are we going, Mara?" His tone, so somber, so full of dread.

"I need to visit my friend before the snow flies. You never know when it's going to come this time of year." My voice shook.

There was still time to turn around. This errand felt dirty, but Wes had to know how much his father meant to me—and how much he still meant to Wes.

I'd been honest when I'd said I didn't agree with how Sam had reacted to Wes after the divorce. He'd never come out and said it, but Wes's mother was indeed a nasty, selfish person.

Still, I didn't feel much better than Jennifer Robson as I drove under the wrought-iron archway into the cemetery.

Wes had fallen quiet, his mouth clamped shut. His hand twitched like he was going to open the door and dive out with a tuck and roll.

Having been here only once, I found my way without getting lost. His headstone, more like a monument, was in place. It hadn't yet been erected the last time I'd visited.

I parked with my headlights not directly on Sam's resting place. "Are you coming out?"

His stricken gaze was glued to the towering gray masterpiece. "Why would I? I didn't know him."

Except the pain in his words sounded fresh and torn from his soul.

Tears prickled my eyes as I walked to the grave. The visit brought clarity as if Sam spoke in my ear that Wes's actions had to do with Sam and not me directly.

"What do I do, Sam?" I whispered. A tear rolled down my cheek.

My friend had been so good at advice, spilling it readily to all who'd listen. A product of his years of being in a leadership position.

I glanced over my shoulder. Wes's head was down. This had to be killing him.

"Why didn't you tell him? Why'd you cut him off entirely?" Why'd I get dragged into the middle?

There were no answers from the grave.

Wes

I POKED AT MY FOOD. Unappetizing macaroni coated in yellow-dyed powder was soaked in half a cow's worth of butter. When Chef made mac and cheese, it was the stuff a five-star restaurant could serve with pride.

Sam's grave.

My stomach turned. What had possessed her to go to Sam's fucking grave?

Mara's gaze was on me, but I wouldn't look at her. I couldn't decide if I was furious with her, numb, or should drink a liter of whiskey and crawl inside the bottle.

She set her fork down. "Are you done?"

I nodded and she took our plates to the sink.

"Did you…did you fix my sink?"

"Yeah," I said hoarsely. "I had a friend help me." Without Flynn, I'd have gotten nowhere. "Hope you don't mind. We also fixed the bathroom sink and the cupboard doors." She jerked around to look for sure. "And we sealed the windows for winter."

"Wow." She stared at the sink with a stunned expression and my chest threatened to puff with pride. "Thank you. Your friend's kind of handy to have around."

The corner of my mouth lifted at her teasing. "He's not a bad guy." A swell of emotion hit me. I liked pleasing her, liked making her life easier, liked joking around with her. Confusion morphed into remorse and the combo churned the processed food in my belly. I pushed back from the table before he did something stupid like confess everything. "Listen, I'm going to have to get going. I hope you don't mind."

Disappointment creased her brow. "Is everything okay?"

"It'll be fine. Just not feeling well." I went in search of my duffel and grabbed my coat, not bothering to put it on.

She met me at the front door. I dropped a light kiss on her lips before I left, the worry in her eyes haunting me.

The drive home felt longer than normal. I never looked forward to going home, not like when I went to Mara's place.

My house was empty. I pulled into my four-car garage, relieved that my mom hadn't taken root while I'd been gone.

I took the stairs at an easy pace and dropped my duffel by the laundry basket. The clothes I'd worn with Flynn were dirty. Flynn had made the crack that I could wash them at Mara's because he knew full well I had never run a washer in my life.

In the upper level where I spent the majority of my time, I bypassed my home office and the master bedroom and went to the door at the end of the hall.

I flipped on the light and faced tubs full of toys and cardboard boxes full of comics. When I'd been shipped off to boarding school on the East Coast, my mom had put them all into storage. A move unusual for my mother, who was more likely to burn things than store them. But even my mom had expressed rare sympathy for how Sam had abandoned me.

For hours, I sifted through old comics while memories assaulted me. I wondered if that old comic book store was still open.

A quick search on my phone revealed that it'd been closed for ten years. Years after the divorce. Had Sam gone in until the day the doors had shut? If he had, had he remembered how much fun we used to have? No less than once a month, we'd collected the latest comics.

I pulled out Sam's old Star Wars comics. I ran my hand over the plastic cover booklet and recalled Sam's gruff voice bitching about how the comics in those days weren't canon and strayed from the origins of the Star Wars universe.

I smiled despite the sharp pain in my chest. It was why I'd named my night club Canon.

With a frustrated sigh, I shoved all the books back in place and glared at the piles of toys. I'd completely unravel if I cracked the lid of any of those.

My phone rang and I expected Mara to be calling, but it was Helen. I frowned. This late on a Saturday? I couldn't let it go to voicemail.

"Mr. Robson, I need to meet with you about the findings I have on Miss Baranski."

"Meet you at the office in the morning? Ten o'clock?"

"I'll be there."

I hung up and put my head in my hands. Meeting tonight would've been best, but my intuition said I should try to get some rest first.

CHAPTER 17

es

I DRESSED and drove to my office tower. Helen waited outside and I let us in.

"We don't need to mess with going upstairs. Have a seat in the vestibule, Helen."

Brusque and to the point, she laid out a folder of papers. "I didn't have to dig very deep, sir. Two major concerns popped out immediately."

She handed me a form and I scanned the print, my eyes narrowing as I read.

"Is this a trust?"

"From one William Kostopoulos to Mara Baranski. One point five million dollars when she turned twenty-two."

"What's the relation? Or was it a relationship?"

She crossed her penny loafers at the ankle and leaned in. "Mind you, the financial department hasn't dug that far yet. However, I found no marriage certificate for her mother so I assume Baranski is a maiden name. Again, nothing is proven, but something I felt you should know since this seemed an urgent matter."

I set the paper down, my heart thundering. "If that's the first, I'd hate to see the second."

Helen's entire demeanor changed to disapproving and not directed toward me. "Academic records." She handed me more sheets. I read the report, but my brain refused to comprehend the gravity of it all.

"Her last semester and she was failing a critical class needed for her degree. Odd because all her other grades had been decent. She could never claim summa cum laude, but she did all right. Yet she never finished, not at that college."

Yep. I'd gotten to that part. An ocean rushed through my ears, dimming Helen's explanation.

"Miss Baranski, perhaps thinking one point five wasn't enough for her to live on, wanted to graduate, so she struck a deal with Dr. Jake Johannsen. They both scored in a way. His wife caught wind and went to the administration. Mara left the school with no degree and Dr. Johannsen got divorced."

Mara was a home-wrecker.

My hands curled into fists. My comic book shop owner had destroyed another man's life before going after my father.

How the fuck had she gotten a trust with that amount of money? What had she done for that? *Who* had she done for that?

The papers shook in my hand. Helen clasped her hands on her lap, her back erect. "We have more investigating, but I thought perhaps this could put that legal nonsense to rest."

"Yes, Helen. Thank you. You may go. Enjoy your Sunday." One of us should.

She left me with the incriminating evidence.

I tossed the papers onto the chair next to me and threw

my feet on top of the table. Surrounded by glass and all alone, I stretched out and ruminated.

My phone rang.

Jennifer. My mom. I could answer and ask her how a woman could do that to men. But then she'd get ideas. Worse, she'd sniff out another woman trying to get her claws into Sam's empire. I pitied any future wife of mine—not that I would ever marry.

I rubbed my temples. What had I expected? These reports were exactly the reason I'd hooked up with Mara.

So, what? It made me feel better that Sam had been seduced by Mara and hadn't preferred a stranger to his own son?

Did I have anything to drink in my office? A day getting shit-faced sounded divine.

My phone rang again. I stared at the ceiling. During the shittiest five minutes of my life, no one was going to leave me alone.

I glanced at the screen. Franklin.

Let the good news rain down.

"What's up?"

"Mr. Robson. We're hitting some obstacles with the permits in New York. I think you should be there in person tomorrow to resolve them."

Fucking New York and the mess it was turning out to be. Flying there used to be a pleasant change, now it was a nuisance. "I'll fly out tonight. Send the info."

I hung up on Franklin. If I weren't such a control freak, I'd let Helen handle Franklin and New York. It'd serve the old boy right.

A long flight with nothing but my fury to keep me company.

Unless...

I punched in Mara's number. "You awake?"

She chuckled. "It's almost noon. I'm on my way to see Mom. Are you feeling better?"

I grimaced. Her concern sounded genuine. She was good. "I've got special plans for tonight. We're going out and it's a surprise."

"But—"

"Saying no isn't allowed. Have I got a surprise for you. I'll pick you up at five."

I heard the smile in her voice when she finally said yes.

Yeah. I had a surprise, all right.

∼

Mara

GIDDY BUTTERFLIES DANCED in my stomach as I raced out to meet Wes. How long had he been parked out there? I'd expected him to come to the door. I'd happened to peek out and had seen him sitting and staring straight ahead, his profile barely discernible in the fading daylight.

When I crawled in, I gulped at the predatory look he gave me. Streetlights gleamed over his dark hair and shadows shaded his eyes. His dark green Henley and black jeans added to the sinister effect.

"Ready for the surprise?"

My first instinct was to say no. The change from how he'd left last night to this set off faint alarms. "Absolutely."

He leaned over and brushed my lips with his. "You'll have to wait." With a wink, he tore off.

He didn't talk much so I tried to guess what he had planned. When he started slowing down and making turns, I couldn't believe it.

"The airport?"

He grinned. "Just wait."

I'd never flown anywhere, none of it was familiar, but he seemed to be driving places most normal people wouldn't.

What was he pulling?

He parked in a small lot. "Come on."

He pulled me out in the brisk air and I had to trot to keep up with the hold he had on my hand.

A small white plane with blue lines sat with blinking lights. A small set of stairs ran down from an open door.

"Sam?"

His smile didn't reach his eyes. "Surprise."

He hustled me inside and my eyes widened at the sophisticated cabin. What style would my old friend have called this? Business mogul contemporary?

A man in a pilot's uniform shut us into the plane and my chest squeezed in a burst of claustrophobia. He avoided looking at them as he disappeared into the cockpit.

Wes settled me into a puffy leather chair, and as I stared around me, not sure if I should be thrilled, or scared, or both, he buckled me in. Somehow, I heard the click over my pounding heart. Wes sat next to me and buckled himself in.

I craned my neck over the seats. There was no one else on the flight. This plane and the way it screamed *make it rain* fit the image of Wes's headshot, the one Ephraim had shown me. Modern, upscale. I could imagine him in a suit by a designer I couldn't afford to hear the name of, relaxed in a chair, swirling a glass of the Macallan he'd ordered the night we'd met.

The Wes I pictured in this plane, looming in that office tower by Arcadia, was not the Wes I'd come to know, the Wes I *thought* I'd known.

A man's voice filled the cabin from a hidden speaker. "Sir, prepare for takeoff."

Wes leaned over. "I promised to cover all the safety measures with you in order to fly with minimal crew."

"What's going on?" A tendril of unease snaked through me. A man who was pretending to be another man was stealing me away at night on a private jet.

Mothers everywhere probably felt like it was too absurd to warn their daughters about situations like this.

"Sam?"

He did a double-take at the tremor in my voice and asked in an incredulous tone, "You're not scared, are you?"

"You have a private jet?"

His expression shut down. "Business is good." He shrugged, his tone flat. "What can I say?"

I squeezed my eyes shut. I was so in over my head. He'd grown up manipulating people. What had I been thinking when I'd thought to fool him? Confronting him as soon as O found out was what I should've done. Hindsight shows the target on a fool's ass, old Sam had always said.

"I'll save the real surprise for when we're in the air."

My fingers curled to unhook my seatbelt as panic threatened to set in. "Take me back."

The plane lurched forward and I gripped my seat, white-knuckling it through taxiing. His hand landed on top of mine.

"Relax." His voice was surprisingly soft. "I have some business in New York, but I had something really important to talk with you about. Two birds, one stone, and all that."

As the plane sped up and the roar of the engine grew louder, I gulped, not wanting to be one of the birds he was dealing with.

He held my hand all through takeoff until the cabin light dinged that it was safe to move around.

He unbuckled himself and stood. "Lemme show you around."

I got to my feet and discovered my knees were wobbly. I didn't fear Wes. He might be a monster in business, but while this situation and how he was acting sent warning flares up left and right, he would never physically hurt me. Seduce me, yes. Fly me to a strange city... We were flying to *New York*? I had to work in the morning. Could I use my cell phone to call Chris and see if he could open?

"If you have to use the facilities, it's that door there."

I spotted the narrow lavatory door.

He swirled his hand where he stood by a glossy wooden table surrounded by four plush chairs. "This is my meeting room. Where we sit during takeoff and landing or when we want to ignore each other."

"We?"

"My staff." His piercing blue eyes pinned me in place. "If you want a drink, we have a fully stocked wet bar."

A glass of something strong sounded appealing.

I forced my feet to move. "I need to use the restroom."

Shuffling past him, I kept my gaze riveted to the red-carpeted floor with each step instead of on him.

"You don't look well. There's a bedroom beyond the toilet, if you need to lay down—after we talk."

I closed my eyes and paused briefly. Wes Robson had a private bedroom in his private plane. How charming. Was it an exclusive club of women that got to be in it?

Why did it break my heart to think of him dallying with others in this plane?

The lavatory made my bathroom look gloriously spacious. I leaned on the pristine sink counter, all two inches of it, and stared at my reflection.

What was Wes up to? What had changed for him to *surprise* me? How much more could he do to me other than take my livelihood away?

I took a fortifying breath and unlatched the door.

"I didn't think you were ever coming out." He took a step toward me, the familiar heat in his gaze. "Do you feel like lying down?"

"No," I said abruptly. No matter what he was up to, I'd turn to putty as soon as he touched me.

He stepped back, calm mask back in place. "Okay. So... have a seat."

I chose a plush chair on the opposite side of the table from him. He took a seat.

We watched each other, like poker players not knowing what the other's hand held.

I glanced out the window. Nothing but black sky. "How long is the flight?"

"About two more hours."

"Then New York, huh?"

"Excited?"

"I have no money, no luggage. And I work in the morning." I ran my hands up and down what had to be leather armrests. When he didn't reply, I struggled to find a neutral topic. "How was your day?"

A haughty lift of a brow. "Informative. And yours?"

"Fine. I had a nice visit with my mom."

His right eye twitched. "How is Wendy?"

"She's well. I haven't told her I'm losing the store. Stress isn't good for her."

Another near wince. Could I appeal to his sensitivities?

"Why don't you open another store again?"

"Money. Not all of us have it."

"But you do."

"Pardon?"

He reached down to a briefcase and withdrew a folder. "You have, in fact, over a million dollars."

I quit stroking the chair. He'd said his day was informative. Now I knew why. And this was how he wanted to talk about it, by mixing me in with New York business.

"What's this about, Wes?"

"It's about—" His steel gaze glared at me as it dawned on him what name I'd used. He reclined, a mask of calm in place. "I guess I don't need to introduce myself. You continue to be full of surprises."

My hands twisted on my lap. "I didn't know who you were until last Saturday when you visited the store. One of the guys recognized you and enlightened me as to who my new boyfriend was."

"Boyfriend?" His voice filled with derision. "Were we exclusive?"

Ouch. Like a rabbit punch to the sternum.

"I was," I said in a ragged whisper.

His only tell was the muscle jumping in his jaw. "And you happily played along."

"I wanted to show you how normal people lived since you seem to think I did something so atrocious."

Rage clouded his features. "Do normal people stop at cemeteries with their new boyfriends? That was dirty, Mara."

I swallowed. He was correct, it'd been a desperate move and one that probably had torn him apart.

"Sam was my friend and I miss him. I thought you'd finally see how much he meant to me and that I wasn't using him."

"You seduced him."

"I did not. And I resent that because I have breasts, you think I'd use them to get what I want in life. Do you do that when you're working? Have sex to get a contract?"

His expression turned incredulous. Well, there was that about him. His work ethic didn't cross the line even if he did in other ways.

"Sam and I were friends."

He barked out a laugh. "I have a good friend and at no time have I ever thought to offer him any of my properties or holdings for a mere dollar."

The tension drained out of me. He didn't believe me and countered with arrogant confidence every point I made. So, this was the real Wes. The man people faced in the boardroom. The guy a whole neighborhood in New York despised.

"Is your friend on the brink of losing his home and the care his mother needs?"

"He works for a living."

I recoiled like I'd been slapped. "I work hard for what I have."

He flung a sheet of paper across the table. "Except for the cool million that was given to you."

I scooted to the edge of my chair to double-check the paper. "My trust? Is that what you're talking about?"

"Who's William Kostopoulos?"

I stood up and threw the sheet back at him. He flinched but the paper only fluttered to the floor. "My grandfather."

The cabin wasn't large, but I had a good five steps to pace in anger.

"Your mom was never married. He's not a Baranski."

I planted my hands on my hips and faced him, leaning forward. "Have your people do a better job. My mom took her stepdad's name. My grandparents divorced when she was a baby. My grandma remarried and they moved out of Greece. Grandpa Kostopoulos died when I was young, but he distributed his wealth to all his grandkids, me, and the ones from his second wife. I told you I had a soft spot for Greece. Arcadia? Get it? As for the money, I used some to open the store and the rest is going to pay for Mom's treatments and nursing home care."

His only reaction was the slight narrowing of his eyes. My grandparents' story didn't move him? My use of the money? Good grief, the real Wes was intimidating. And heartless.

"Cornering me in this plane was despicable."

He didn't stand but leaned forward in his chair. "Me? Between you and Sam, I don't know who makes me more sick."

Not even a raised voice and here I was quivering from hurt and anger.

"Sam loved you. And I didn't seem to make you sick all those times we had sex."

He lifted a shoulder. "Occupational hazard."

I blew out an exaggerated puff of air. My heart seized like a vice had tightened around it with the stark realization he in no way cared for me. At all.

"Explain why an old man latches onto a woman in her early twenties."

"He had no children that spoke to him and I had no father."

"Still with the 'just friends' story?" He reached back into that damn case and extracted two more papers.

He had more on me. My heart hammered and dread rose. Please, no.

"What about Dr. Jake Johannsen? Were you two just friends? His wife—excuse me, ex-wife—didn't think so."

My face grew cold as the blood drained from it. He went there. Took my nightmare and used it against me.

"Jake was a sexual predator."

"Was that why you fucked him for a better grade?"

Hot tears rolled down my face. "Did you see the rest of my grades? As and Bs. Did you ask yourself why I was suddenly failing? Because I certainly didn't understand. And maybe I would've thought about it if my mom hadn't been so sick and if I hadn't been making myself sick trying to care for her."

Wes settled back and crossed one leg over the other and clasped his hands in front of his stomach.

At least he was willing to listen.

"I couldn't afford more school. I didn't know about my grandfather's trust because I was still twenty-one and I wasn't supposed to get it until I turned twenty-two. Mom didn't tell me partly because she didn't believe it herself and partly because she knew I'd use the money for her."

I paced. Tears dripped onto my shirt. "Then Jake was all 'let's talk in my office' and he was so understanding. I poured my heart out to him. He didn't wear a wedding ring, you know. No pictures around the office."

I didn't quit moving. Wouldn't look at Wes. I hadn't told anyone but my therapist what had happened.

"I didn't plan to sleep with him. I wasn't interested. Then May rolled around and I was sitting five points below a D. 'D for degree', right? I was so desperate. He listened to me, kept telling me it'd be okay. And I let my guard down and he made his move. I said no, but he said he wanted to help, and I was smart enough to know I wouldn't pass if I didn't have sex with him."

I shoved my bangs out of my face. "He was a handful of years older than me so I didn't think it'd hurt anyone else. Then he kept wanting it, and there were only two more weeks of school. I just had to make it two more weeks and I'd be done and get the passing grade." All those emotions rolled back. Humiliation, stupidity, the shame. Turned out I still hated myself for it. "But he had a wife and she found out what his late hours meant and she gunned for me hard. I couldn't blame her."

Drawing in a ragged breath, I faced Wes, who hadn't moved. "I'm certain he tampered with my grade, and I even made the accusation, but the wife had more pull than I did. I didn't graduate and was looking for a job when we got news of the money from my grandfather."

"Convenient explanations, all of them." His lip curled in disgust.

Her temper snapped. "What do you want, Wes?" I shouted and abruptly lowered my volume. "I'm not the villain. I had a successful and generous grandfather and a piece of shit professor. Sam had no friends. All he had were memories of his time with you."

"Yet he spent all his time with you."

"So. What," I spat.

"Do you know how much that strip mall is worth?"

I flung my hands out. "I don't give a shit."

"Tens of millions."

Much of my anger drained. "Bullshit. It's a run-down, old building."

"Look what it's surrounded by. I quoted list price. It would've assessed at much more. You were going to fleece Sam for millions. Oh, I'm sorry. Twenty-nine million, nine hundred ninety-nine thousand, nine hundred, and ninety-nine dollars."

"He wanted to help me because he knew you wouldn't," I hissed. "You're too much like your mother."

Wes shot out of his chair. "I am nothing like her."

He glared at me and stalked around the table. I backed up and with startling clarity realized it wasn't because I was scared, but because the real Wes was more potent than watered-down Wes.

"I'm sure Sam told you a lot in your time together." His tone was ice.

"He did. Because that's what friends do. Unlike you, he supported me."

"It's what men around you seem to do. Support you a whole lot."

I reared back. "You're talking about my *grandfather*."

Now Wes's hands were planted on his hips and he towered over me. "I'll have to verify who he was to you."

"I don't care."

"Regardless, your track record *with a professor* doesn't shine a positive light on your relationship with Sam."

"I was taken advantage of." I bit out each word.

"So you decided to do the same to an old man? You're a millionaire and it wasn't good enough for you."

"Are you serious? How far do you think a million will go if my mom lives ten years? Twenty years?" I choked back a sob because I doubted her mom would make it that long. "And let's see, factor in *at least* two hospital stays each year, plus her medication? I'll be lucky if that money lasts a decade."

Wes's attention was zeroed on me, but for once, he seemed to consider my explanation.

I swiped at my eyes. "I'm glad you met my mom because you probably wouldn't even believe I have one."

His right eye twitched.

"Oh my god. You *didn't* believe I had a sick mom?" I blinked. I pulled my shoulders back and straightened. "And after we started dating? Has nothing I've done convinced you that I'm not a leech?"

Like that, the hardness snapped back into his gaze and he cocked his head. "You mean when you were willing to sleep with me hours after we met?"

"You were the same, only you were *lying* about who you were. Again, is it worse because I have boobs?"

His livid gaze dropped to my chest. Right eye twitch. "What I witnessed, dating you, was a woman who whined about her store being shut down, but did nothing to secure work in the entire forty-five days I gave you."

"A month and a half to replace my sole revenue stream

that took years to build?" I threw my hands up. "How generous of you, Wes. And as for going out and getting a job, do you know how much anxiety I have at the thought of being coerced by another person? I've been looking for women-led companies, but that doesn't guarantee my supervisor won't be a man. I couldn't even partner with Chris on a new location."

Wes had a *does not compute* look to him.

"Yes, Wes. A *man* offered to help me and I turned him down. And as for why you didn't see me applying for jobs, it's because you were trying to get into my bed every time we were together."

That snapped him into a defensive posture. "There were no arguments from you. And I have no doubt that you would've been digging into my wallet eventually."

With one hand on my hip, I pinched the bridge of my nose with the other. There was no getting through to him. Not after he'd dated the real me and still thought I was a shallow freeloader.

"What was all this about?" I dropped my hand to look at him. "Why *surprise* me with a trip to New York and not reveal your lurid findings at my place?"

His jaw worked and I wondered if he even knew the answer. "Because I had to come here for work and I wasn't going to sit and let you plot while I was gone. You're running out of time."

"I'm aware."

"Despite how even more men are willing to help you otherwise."

"More men? Are you talking about Ephraim? Then I guess you're right. He offered and I took him up on it. No sex involved, FYI. The city council," I wasn't going to shine a light on Chris though Wes could probably guess who was behind it, "well, that's a woman, and you pissed her off all on your own. In fact, Ephraim's not so much helping me but going after a greedy, emotionless, conscienceless corporate tycoon who doesn't give a damn about anyone without enough zeroes behind their name."

"None of it will work. I'm still putting you out of business and ripping down that piece of shit your store is in."

"I'm learning not to expect much more from you."

"Sit down and enjoy the rest of the flight, Mara. You'll have to find your own way home."

Wha— A pit bloomed in her stomach. "You're leaving me in a strange city in the middle of the night?"

"I'm sure some guy will come along and be willing to rescue you. Seems to be your thing."

He had all the power and I was helpless, stuck thousands of feet in the air. My eyes locked on the seat the farthest away from him and I staggered to it. Before I collapsed in it to cry silently to myself, I turned back.

"By the way, my mom asked about you, wanted to know how you were doing."

Another wince.

On the bright side, we'd fought most of the flight and I didn't have to wait long to land.

I supposed Wes would want me to get off first. Ugh, I didn't want to face him.

Don't let him break your heart.

Sorry, Mom.

The plane touched down while I clutched the armrests. We taxied for a few minutes before coming to a stop. I'd come up with a game plan through my haze. I had my debit card and license. How much would a ticket cost? As long as there were signs pointing me to a ticket counter, I'd find my way home.

What if private jets landed in an entirely different area?

No matter. I'd foot the bill for a ride.

I unbuckled and clutched my purse. Wes walked down the aisle. His ominous presence warranted a long black cape billowing behind him to the beat of "The Imperial March."

One of the pilots appeared and Wes spoke a few words to him. Then the door opened with a burst of cold air and he disappeared.

Not even a look back. And I'd hoped for what?

For Wes to not be the heartless prick he'd been the last hour, to show me some of the guy who'd tucked me in and curled up behind me.

Would it matter? He'd proved what he was capable of.

I pushed up, but the pilot Wes had spoken to walked toward me.

"Ms. Baranski, Mr. Robson made arrangements for us to return you home."

I stomped my relief down but made a quick, rash decision. "I appreciate it, but all I'd like are directions to where I can buy a commercial plane ticket."

Confusion registered in the man's expression, with a touch of worry. "I'm sorry?"

"Mr. Robson has made it clear how he feels about me accepting anyone's generosity. Thank you. I'm sure it's been a long night for you as well."

"But Ms. Baranski—"

"Excuse me." I skirted around him but stalled on the first step. Lights from buildings and planes surrounded me and I could make out little in the dark.

"Are you sure, ma'am?"

"Positive."

He rattled off what I had to do to get to a ticket counter and I was on my way.

CHAPTER 18

 es

I RELAYED THE STORY. Exhaustion weighed me down. The whirlwind and stress of business in New York, the flight delay back due to a storm, all piled onto sleepless nights.

Flynn listened with ever-rising eyebrows.

We sat in Canon's office on a Friday night. I always kept my door shut, but tonight it guarded against the beat of the music that would add to my pounding headache.

"She didn't let you fly her back?"

"Nope." I recalled my pilot's worried recounting of Mara's refusal and the man's resentment at being put in the situation of ditching a young woman in the middle of the night in an unfamiliar city. Guess I deserved it.

"What if she's telling the truth about everything?"

"Are you on her side?" My friend's hypothetical question was the same one that had been running through my mind all week.

"Look at you, Wes. Bloodshot eyes, wrinkled clothes. If you thought she was a money whore, you'd be out on the floor, picking up your entertainment for tonight."

I stared at the floor. "She got to me, that's all. She's that good."

"Good enough to get her grandpa to leave her money," Flynn said dryly.

I flipped him off. "I wasn't talking about that." And Helen had warned me she didn't have all the facts. "The professor, Sam, her employee, and her customers. She's a user."

"Yeah, maybe." Flynn's tone wasn't his usual confident one. "I don't like seeing you like this. I'm worried about you, bro."

"Don't be. I'll get over it." I refused to admit that I'd fallen for Mara, but my words came close.

"I was going to tell you to get out there and get back in the saddle." Flynn leaned forward and whispered, "Bachelorette party. But," he returned to concerned friend, "I don't want you to do something stupid like elope with a fling because you have a broken heart."

I made a *pssht* sound. "I don't have a broken heart. I don't like her."

"Mm-hmm. In case I didn't mention a bachelorette party, there's one out there now and it's calling me. Nothing like the always-a-bridesmaid-never-a-bride hookup." Flynn left, but I didn't miss the *holy shit, dude, you're a sad sack and I'm worried about you* glance.

I dove into my work. Pouring over shipment notices and orders, I was finally at a point where Mara wasn't dominating my thoughts when my office phone rang.

"Boss," his bartender said, "there's a hot chick here asking about you."

I was out of my office in seconds and weaving through

the throng of people to the bar. What I saw when I approached slowed me to a halt.

No Mara. Just Hailey in leggings and a low-slung top. With a frustrated grunt, I spun around and slammed back into my office.

∼

Mara

I SAT in my half-empty office and dabbed my eyes. It was the last game day. Chris had brought donuts again. Ephraim and Joe had each brought food and they'd lined up a goodbye potluck that had lasted until closing time.

Choking on the overwhelming sense of loss, I'd escaped to my office.

I hadn't heard from Wes all week. Hadn't expected to and had deleted his contact info from my phone.

"Mara?" Chris called from the other side.

"Come in." Who cared if he saw me crying?

He pushed open my door and his smile was understanding, and, dammit, I'd miss him.

"I've been working on a proposal and looking for space. I...I emailed you a proposal if you'd seriously consider partnering with me."

"Oh god, Chris." I scrubbed my eyes and cursed Wes for the eight-hundredth time in a week. If he hadn't dragged my past through a mud pit, I might have considered Chris's offer. "I'm really sorry. I don't want to hold you back."

"I understand, but take a look and if things change, we'll talk."

"I appreciate you not giving up on this place."

He shrugged and cut a hand through his shaggy hair. "A

well-run comic store is hard to find. What you did with this place in less than three years is astounding. You have a good sense for business."

"I'd like to claim the success, but you and customers like Ephraim helped me a lot." And Sam with his keen intellect and business experience.

"No one ever does it by themselves. Don't sell yourself short, Mara. You're the one who led this operation and made the decisions."

"You don't know how much I needed to hear that." The complete opposite of the entire flight to New York.

He looked regretfully toward the rest of the store. "I can't believe next week is our last week. I guess I'll see you Monday."

"I'll walk out with you."

We wished each other a good weekend in the parking lot and then I was on my way home for a long night of job hunting and filling out applications.

CHAPTER 19

es

I STARED at the empty lot. The Heart of Downtown Mall was closed.

The steep satisfaction I'd expected forty-five days ago was absent.

Mara hadn't tried calling me. No pleas for forgiveness, no fuck you, nothing but radio silence. As if I'd expected anything else.

The weekend had been so utterly boring and here it was Friday and I faced another.

Because I must be a masochist, I'd watched the entire run of Star Wars. Flynn had even popped in for a few movies. He'd left, saying he could feel his butt flattening as each new movie started.

My driver texted me, asking if I needed a ride. Poor guy. He was starting to worry about his job. I kept driving the hybrid around. One day, I'd tell Helen to sell it, but for now, I...just couldn't.

No point in staring at an empty building.

I took the stairs down to the ground floor because if Helen could track her steps and never use the elevator, I wasn't about to push a button.

The building receptionist was just picking up her bag. She threw me her thousand-watt smile. "Got exciting plans for the weekend, Mr. Robson?"

"Absolutely," I lied. "Have all keys been turned in from the Heart of Downtown?"

"Two of the three. Arcadia's keys haven't been turned in yet."

I inclined my head in acknowledgment and walked out into air as cold as my soul felt.

∼

Mara

MY STORE WAS OFFICIALLY CLOSED. Arcadia was no more. Technically, I didn't have to be out until Monday. But I had interviews arranged all next week, so I was determined to clear out during the weekend. And since my visits with my mom were on Sundays, I'd spent my Saturday moving.

A week ago, the place had been hopping with people and laughter. My lineup of gaming systems that hadn't sold waited to be packed in the scattered boxes and hauled out. Between eBay and Craigslist, I planned to sell what hadn't moved before the final shutdown yesterday.

I went to push my bangs out of my eyes, but my hand fell to my side. How long to break the habit? Just before I'd come to the store, I'd had a hair appointment—no more pink, and a new sleek cut. I still had bangs, but they had been shortened and tapered into the rest of my hair, which fell to my shoulders. They'd cut a good three inches off but I could still do ponytails. I planned to finish hauling boxes home so that after my visit on Sunday I could look for professional clothing.

After one load, I returned to the store and lifted more boxes and any small shelves I could fit into my car. I'd asked Chris to take as much of the furniture as possible, otherwise it'd have to stay and go down with the building. Or get sold and added to Wes's massive fortune.

So, it'd go down with the store.

"Aw, man." My favorite Batman leggings had a tiny hole. Perfect symbolism. Everything I loved was being destroyed.

Making a slow circle, I considered whether I should try to load more. Some of the items were just too large and too heavy. Chris had said he'd filled his garage. So what was left was likely going to stay.

The front door chimed and a sense of alarm raced through me. I'd backed my car as close as possible to use the bigger door, but I should've locked it.

I wheeled around and my heart stopped at the last gorgeous man on earth I wanted to see. "What are you doing here?"

Wes's gaze swept over me and settled on my forehead. "What the fuck happened to your hair?"

It looked nice! I patted it to make sure no strands were out of place. "Pink doesn't scream young professional and I need every advantage during my interviews. What are you doing here?"

"You didn't return the keys."

"I have until Monday. Forty-five days."

His brows drew down for a millisecond. Hadn't thought of that, had he?

He wandered around the store. Did he see the same desolation I did?

I studied his outfit. A CEO's version of business casual. His slacks draped perfectly to his expensive shoes, and his pristine shirt was unbuttoned at the neck. No tie and the sleeves were rolled up. No coat despite the dropping October temps, but then he didn't have far to go to track down the keys.

I spun to the counter that used to house action figures and advertisements for Comic-Cons but was now empty and collecting dust. The keys rested on the top. I snatched them up, but when I turned, I plastered myself against the counter.

Wes stood a foot away. "Your leggings have a hole."

"That happens." I hated the breathless quality to my voice. Hate was too strong of a term, but extreme disappointment and serious dislike were adequate.

"You got home okay?"

"Obviously."

His gaze caressed my face like he couldn't get used to my grown-up look. "How much did the ticket cost?"

"More than I'd planned to spend. But thanks to Grandpa Kostopoulos, I covered it."

The blue of his eyes darkened a shade. "Why didn't you just take the damn plane home?"

I pushed off the counter and poked his rock-hard chest. "You know why."

He crowded me into the counter and placed his hands on either side. "It wasn't a test. You should've let them fly you home."

I refused to cower, which wasn't hard when he smelled divine. Not cologne, I'd noticed he never fussed with the stuff, but whoever washed his clothes chose good detergent.

And I knew what he looked like naked. Gloriously naked and aroused and geez, it wasn't helping.

His head dropped lower, but I wouldn't retreat. My eyes were glued to his lips.

"You didn't fire the pilots or anything, did you?" I asked.

"Why would I do that? I'm not unreasonable."

I raised an eyebrow and meant to look around the room, but he covered the distance between us and captured my mouth.

Holy Batman, how was I going to resist him? I held him to me by his collar and he deepened the kiss. His taste was as good as imprinted on my brain.

His hands gripped my waist and lifted me to the counter.

No, I was going to end it. Flattening my hands against his chest, I meant to push him away, but his hands drifted up my shirt to cup my heavy breasts and they all but screamed at me to let him keep going.

Our tongues clashed, movements growing more desperate. I couldn't pull away so I poured my anger into our kiss. Without breaking contact, he reached down to shove my left shoe off, and together we wrestled to get my leggings down. Only one leg was necessary without a shoe to block. I slid my leg free.

Cool glass pressed against my ass. His tongue swirled against mine as his hand cupped my sex. His thumb found my clit and rubbed.

The time we'd been apart felt like years of abstinence. I clawed at the clasp of his slacks. He didn't release me to help but held me close.

Freeing his shaft, I tilted my pelvis. He released my sex to shove inside and immediately started thrusting.

My whine was needy and turned into a moan. Between his embrace and my legs wrapped around him, I was pressed against him so tight, I marveled he could move his hips.

My climax rushed closer. I opened my mouth to pant. He

did the same. Our lips were touching, but we were breathing into each other, using each other for support.

"Oh god, Wes."

His shoulders went rigid before he pumped harder and it dawned on me, it was the first time I'd called out his real name during sex.

I crested and clutched his shoulders. "Yes!"

He growled my name.

His hot release spilled inside of me.

I gasped and my eyes flew open wide. His did the same.

He looked down to where we were connected and panic raced through his expression. Mine probably matched.

"You poison my thinking."

If real venom formed his words, I'd be more hurt than I was. But I'd been thinking the same about him.

"I'm sure it's fine. Wrong time of the month."

The doubt on his face was more hurtful than saying I was poisonous.

I sighed and scooted back. "I can notify your office when I get my period."

More than a little bitterness touched those words.

He pulled out and stuffed himself back in his pants. I wiggled to the side to rearrange my leggings and pull them up, but he stepped with me.

Craning his neck over his shoulder, he swore. My eyes flew wide. Anyone driving by had gotten a good show. It was night outside and while I only had one row of my fluorescent lights on, it was enough to spotlight us.

Surprisingly, he helped me get my foot into my pants and lifted me down so I could roll them up.

"Thanks," I mumbled.

"This doesn't change anything," he said roughly.

"Didn't think it did." I couldn't meet his gaze as I handed him the keys.

I left him standing at the counter while I hefted the last box and walked out the door for the last time.

Wes

Helen listed dates and times.

A week had passed since that Saturday night with Mara on the counter. No protection. I'd never gone without protection.

It'd been glorious. She'd been all wet heat and her orgasm over my naked flesh was the best I'd ever experienced.

"Sir?"

"Say again." Might as well not pretend I was listening.

"Our legal team worked with the city and the permits are in order. Our demolition date has not changed."

"Fabulous." No one could argue that an upgrade was in order, but…I'd have a hard time watching it get demolished.

"We finished our investigation on Mara Baranski."

I cut a look over my shoulder. "Just leave it on the desk."

The thin file was set down without being opened.

"Was there anything more?" I asked quietly.

"Not really. No prom pictures or news clips. William Kostopoulos was her grandfather. I included financial data for Golden Meadows. I couldn't get ahold of her mom's medical records, obviously, but I printed off some information on multiple sclerosis."

So had I. Wendy Baranski's prognosis was grim.

Helen efficiently packed her materials. "Franklin should be here in fifteen minutes. Is there anything else you need?"

"Have a good night, Helen."

I didn't look through the folder. I knew how much a year

at Golden Meadows cost. Had done the calculations. The trust fund wouldn't last long and that was if Mara didn't use any of it for her living expenses.

I rubbed my chest. Kicking her out of the club that night nearly two months ago would've been best.

Could an old man really be BFFs with a twenty-five-year-old woman?

She'd compared me to my mother.

On cue, my phone rang.

"What, Mom?"

"Is that how you address the woman who birthed you?"

When she's only interested in money, yes. "Are you calling to check on how I'm doing, like a real mom?"

"I know you're doing fine, Wesley. You're my son."

My mouth quirked. Good one. "Was Sam ever…did he go after younger women?"

"Sam never left work long enough to chase women. But he was a man. I'm sure he would've liked them young."

Didn't answer my question.

"What brought that question on? Prospective siblings coming out of the woodwork now that news of his fortune going to you is out?" She chortled. "Little do they know— Well, you should have paternity done before anything."

Little did they know what? "No. I just don't know why he'd cut me off after the divorce but leave everything to me."

My mom went quiet. Unusual for her. I waited for the derogatory dig about my father, but nothing.

"He couldn't get over his bitterness, Wes. It's not your fault."

Color me shocked that my mother had said something halfway meant to comfort me. She'd always blown it off as Sam's reaction to the divorce and taking it out on me. This was the first time I'd believed her.

"Did you hear about the cold front coming through?" she

continued. "We might get snow and it's not even December. Have you thought more about the villa?"

"If you want to do it, go for it." With your own money.

"You know I can't afford it. Wesley, the winters are harder and harder for me to get through."

Wow. She sounded serious.

"And since you never invite me over and never meet me out, I might as well not stay in Minnesota."

Someone knocked on the door. Probably Franklin.

"All right, Mom. I've gotta go. Why don't you stop by sometime this weekend and we'll talk."

I barely got her off the phone without hanging up on her, but not even I hung up on my mom.

"Come on in, Franklin."

Sam's old assistant scurried in. "Good news, Mr. Robson. Johnson, Harwood, and Crest dropped their suit against Robson Industries."

"What?"

Franklin's gray brows shot up. I hadn't sounded happy. Admittedly, my first thought was that I wouldn't see Mara again. She'd be at the proceedings—I'd hoped.

"It's over," Franklin echoed his thoughts. "We must, however, discuss New York."

I listened in a daze, giving a grunt to affirm Franklin's actions. Combined with Helen's earlier news about the city, the dropped lawsuit finalized the last business I had with Mara Baranski.

It was over.

CHAPTER 20

ara

I CLASPED MY SWEATY PALMS. I was perspiring in my new business suit, and dang it, it was dry-clean only. TGIF, though.

Enduring my third interview of the week, I smiled politely and answered every question as confidently as possible. No job history as an executive assistant, but I still had experience.

A glance out the window gave me the view of another twenty-floor office building with a face of glass. So city, so refined. I'd grown up here, but downtown Minneapolis was nothing like the little area I'd lived in.

"You owned your own business?" the woman from the three-person interview panel asked.

"Yes, ma'am." I coveted the woman's bottle of water.

The young man who had to be close to my age asked the next question. "Going from running your place, to helping someone else run a business..."

I hated explaining my work history. Technically, my business hadn't failed. I'd formed a succinct answer early on, lest they think I'd run it into the ground. "I leased space in a building owned by Robson Industries, and when his son took over, he had other plans for the property."

The older woman popped her head up from Mara's papers. "Is that the lot by Mr. Robson's office tower?"

"Yes, ma'am."

She smiled. "What a coincidence. Mr. Robson owns this building, as well."

My smile drooped.

One of the men snorted. "Give him enough time and he'll own half the city."

The interview wrapped up after several more questions and too many "I don't have the answer, but I'll make sure I find out" answers.

I drove home, numb from yet another interview pointing out my lack of experience and a college degree.

I was sadly underqualified for every job I'd interviewed for. Hard work and ambition only went so far. Desperation was pushing out the worry of working for another man who'd take advantage of me.

As soon as I changed into pajamas, I jumped online to research who owned all of the buildings where the companies I'd met with were located. Two out of three.

What if they hired me and Wes found out? Then I'd have to apply at places who were Robson-independent.

Two more meetings set up next week. One was in the same building as another place I'd been in. Owned by Robson Industries.

Was I going to be screening every possible employment opportunity?

Ridiculous. I was an adult and so was he.

Could I blame him? He didn't trust me over Sam, and then I'd made myself a nuisance with the help of Chris and Ephraim. It was over and done—and he held all the power. I refused to cower in the shadow of Wes Robson and let it affect my ability to get a damn job. So I knew who he was. We'd had a relationship. I could talk to him like an adult and he could suck it up. But at least I'd know if I had any limitations in regards to job hunting.

I checked the time. Friday night. Would he be at Canon?

Talking myself out of it wasn't worth the stress during job hunting. I changed into the same outfit I'd worn that first night and with another round of sweaty palms, I drove to Canon.

The same bouncer stood guard and I received a more appreciative look than last time. Must be the hair. It was still pinned up in a French bun and as I passed a mirrored column, my new highlights gleamed under the marquis lights.

Like last time, I went straight to the bar. Same bartender. Could this night get any more déjà vu?

"What'll you have?" He set a coaster in front of me.

"I'll have the pop star's wine and I need to talk to Wes."

He rewarded my courage with a bored blink. "He's not here. I'll get your drink."

As he poured my wine, he got on the phone.

Yes. Wes was at the club.

∼

Wes

. . .

After meeting with Franklin, I had headed to Canon, but since I'd been doing nothing but working, I had nothing to do.

I'm sure playing *League of Legends* on a Friday night was exactly what most twenty-eight-year-olds did. Flynn interrupted his game with a message that he'd be here soon with dinner because I was under orders not to "fuck around" until I had my "sad-sack shit together."

The bartender called. "A hot chick wants to talk to you."

I rolled my eyes. "Is it the desperate blonde again?"

"This one's fine. Better quality than the wine she ordered."

I hung up and stared at the door. Could it be?

When I'd met her, she'd joked about what she was drinking.

With slow precision, I opened my door and walked down the dark hallway to the entrance to the main area.

I stepped out, but the mirrored pillars scattered throughout the place blocked my view. Patrons moved out of my way, but I noticed no one. My gaze swept the bar and I saved the seat I'd first seen her in for last.

The breath whooshed out of my lungs. Her beauty had struck me down before, but the sophisticated lady perched on the barstool, with a hairdo that bared her slender neck, was a work of art.

No more makeup enhanced her features than before. The outfit was the same and while it highlighted all her curves, I preferred her Batman leggings.

I came to a stop behind her, not sitting like before because look how that had turned out. "Mara."

She slowly twisted with a hesitant smile. "Can we talk?"

"About what?"

Her gaze fell from me and she scanned the people around

us. She opened her mouth to talk. No, I craved privacy with her.

"Come with me." I turned, knowing I was fueling staff gossip about the lady I'd brought back to my office.

Once we were behind a closed door, I wondered how she saw the first private environment of mine she'd been in. Modern, sleek, stark, and barren. No personal touches.

No different than my public spaces, like my plane, which certainly hadn't impressed her.

To put space between us, I went around the desk and took a seat. She sat on the edge of the chair Flynn usually used.

"How's job hunting going?"

She grimaced. "I'm here to discuss it."

A fifty-pound weight settled on my chest. She was here to use me.

"I've been interviewing and it was pointed out to me that you own a few of the buildings where I was meeting possible employers. I want to know if that'll be a problem."

The weight lifted.

She held her hand up. "Before you answer, I'm not saying this to sway you, but I want to apologize. I shouldn't have tried to cause problems and delays for you. It was an immature move. With the…history…between us, I want to know beforehand if I should pursue businesses that are free and clear of you."

"It won't be a problem." My guilt flared. She was out of work because of me. "I can call and put in a good word for you."

"Yeah, no. You don't know the first thing about how well I perform at work." She spiked an adorable blush as she said "perform." "And that is the last thing I'd ask of you."

We fell quiet for a few moments.

"How's Wendy?"

"Mom's stable."

"Did you tell her—about everything?"

Mara shook her head. "Stress isn't good for Mom. I gave her a general overview. Funny, because it helped me form a canned response when I'm asked during interviews. I haven't told her we quit seeing each other yet, but I will on my Sunday visit."

So when I suddenly felt like a pile of shit on Sunday, I'd know the reason why. Wendy's learning of my deception didn't sit well with me. "What kind of work are you looking for?"

"Anything. I might pick up a waitressing job while waiting for a higher-paying company with better benefits to hire me."

With my luck with Mara, I'd probably bring a date to the place she worked and get seated in her section. Dating again wasn't appealing, but now it scared me.

"Well." Mara tapped her thighs. "I'd better get going."

I made it to the other side of my desk by the time she rose. "Look, we don't have to…"

Words faded with the hopeless glint in her eyes. "Goodbye, Wes."

My feet were cemented to the floor. She rested her hand on the doorknob and stalled. "There is something else I should talk to you about. It's about Sam."

A cold splash of water. "What about him?"

"We talked, about you, and he never came out and said it, but—"

The door whipped open. Mara stumbled back, losing her balance in her heels. Two steps and I caught her in my arms.

"I've got chow—whoa." Flynn stared at us, stunned while holding two trays.

Mara righted herself and pulled away. "Thank you."

"Hey, Flynn. I'll be right back. I need a minute with Mara." My hand on her back felt too right as I ushered her outside of the office. I shut the door behind me. "Can you come to my place tomorrow?"

Her place was a no, and she'd know why. Too many stupendously erotic memories.

"That guy's your friend?" Suspicion dripped from her words.

I wanted to strangle Flynn for his store visit. "I had no idea he planned to stop in and hit on you. He was just looking out for me."

She shook her head like she couldn't believe it. "Meet at your offices downtown?"

"No, my home." *My cold, barren home.*

Brief hesitation and she nodded. "Text me the address. What time?"

Whatever she wanted to talk to me about overrode her caution about the two of us alone.

I got it. Any longer in my office and I'd repeat the on-the-counter move on my desk.

"Whenever, just let me know."

Her hips swayed all the way down the hall, her shoulders held square. She was miles above any girl in the club.

Dangerous thoughts at a time when she'd finally decided to come clean about Sam. Like I was looking for any excuse to get close to her again and the betrayal mattered less and less.

Steeling myself, I returned to the office.

"You two are talking?" Flynn hadn't made himself comfortable but stood where he'd been when I left.

"Yep." And that was all I was telling Flynn that we'd done.

"You two…"

"She's going to talk to me about Sam tomorrow."

"Uh-huh." Flynn set out the food and utensils. No greasy paper bags from my friend. "She's…classier than last time."

"She lost the edge for job hunting."

"You sound disappointed."

I was.

CHAPTER 21

ara

I DROVE down a long drive with a giant brick mansion capping the end. This was the address he'd sent me. Since his phone number had been seared into my brain, I'd texted him a half hour ago to say I was on my way. Midmorning shouldn't be too early or too late. I'd rather get this over with.

I parked and peered over the steering wheel. Glimmering blue behind the house reflected sunlight with its gentle waves.

He had a *lake*?

Back to the mansion. Much larger now that I was out of the car. Like Wes had told his realtor he wanted the biggest, most pretentious place available. And throw in a private body of water.

I stuffed the small gift I'd brought Wes into my coat

pocket. Deciding when I'd give it to him had plagued me the whole drive.

Elegant stairs rose from the parking area and led to a porch with arches that graced the full length of the house. Precisely manicured shrubs rimmed the perimeter of the porch and the stairs I climbed.

Large, deciduous trees surrounded the property in a ring of protection. Their limbs were bare of leaves this time of year, but I could imagine their beauty in the middle of summer.

An intimidating door waited for me. The mansion could be the Death Star from my trembling hands.

The fear fueling my nerves? That would be Wes kicking a woman out as he invited me in.

Were we exclusive?

The willing bodies populating his club didn't make me feel better, neither did how gorgeous they were. His friend Flynn didn't look like a guy who settled. Between the two of them...

Didn't matter anymore. I'd be done with Wes after our talk today and I wasn't sure I was doing the right thing. Sam had only hinted, never outright said, but we'd talked enough that I'd pieced together the crux of Sam's misery.

As I was staring at the door, wondering if I should knock, ring the bell, or if a formal butler was going to answer, it swung open.

With dismay, I greedily drank in the sight of a shirtless Wes with flannel pants draped low on his waist. Good grief, his body was *sick*.

"Did I wake you?" Stupid question. He'd obviously been waiting for me. I searched behind him, expecting a lingerie-clad hot body to strut by.

"I just finished working out."

Yep, his slicked-back hair was shining from a recent

shower and his designer soap certainly smelled more expensive than my discount bar.

He couldn't get sexier if he paid a cool million for it.

I wore an old coat over a white, oversize T-shirt and leggings that looked like a DC comic wrapped around my skin.

Heat ignited as his gaze swept down my body. "Is that a legit comic?"

He squatted to read my clothes.

"Just a page from Wonder Woman." I shifted my feet. The position we were in set off bursts of stills of us in similar positions.

He straightened, pure hunger radiating from him. "Come in."

He didn't move out of the way to make room for me, crowding me into the wall as he swung the door shut.

The sound echoed off the walls.

"Jeepers, this place is huge."

I pushed past him, rubbernecking like I was in a museum. The atmosphere wasn't much different. The interior design was a clash of old-world elegance and simple modern lines. No ostentatious colors, just earth tones that relaxed the eyeballs, yet didn't invite one to go on in and get cozy.

"Every woman's dream," he said as if the woman would be with him for the house.

I frowned as I wandered out of the foyer and got my first full view of the main room. "Your TV screen is the size of my *car*." I spun in a slow circle. "But no, I'd take my house over this. Except for the bathroom. The coziness of my place with the luxury of just one of the bathrooms in your Bruce Wayne mansion."

"I don't use these areas often." He pointed to the right. "The garages are off the kitchen and the upper level has my bedroom, home office, and family room. I spend most of my time up there."

Not a good idea to step into his intimate domain. "Your Batcave is aboveground."

He chuckled. Holding an arm to the left where the epic screen took up the whole wall, he indicated the plush leather furniture. My ballet flats clicked softly on the tiled floor.

"Oh, wait, your coat." Wes looked around at a loss. "I don't keep the staff around on the weekend."

He has people. For his house. He probably has no idea where to put a coat, plus his gift was in the pocket. "I can just hang onto it."

I shrugged it off and hugged it to me. The depth of the couch prevented me from getting comfortable.

He chose the oversize recliner adjacent to me. "I'm glad you came."

"You might not be after we talk." Just say it. No, I had to lay the groundwork. "When Sam and I first started discussing more than our love of superheroes and sci-fi, naturally we talked about family."

Wes's face turned to stone.

"First, I don't care if you believe me, there was nothing sexual between us. Second, he loved you. So much."

"Then why…"

"Yeah, I'm getting to that. But third," I smiled sheepishly, "I want to make it clear, he never said it in plain words, just beat around the bush—"

"Like you're doing?"

I released a nervous laugh, but Wes didn't crack a smile. "I think what caused the distance between you two is that he found out—"

"Wesley!" a woman's voice called from the direction of the kitchen. "Why did I have to hear from Claudine, who read her husband's emails, that some greedy whore was suing Sam's company?"

Oh. God. My mouth dropped open. Wes briefly closed his eyes as if he couldn't believe the bad timing.

A petite woman I would guess was in her early fifties strode in, her heels click-clacking on the floor. The striking brunette subtly resembled Wes, her identity unmistakable.

"Oh, hello." She stopped and within two seconds, she'd evaluated me.

I touched my forehead, certain a sticker that read "greedy whore" was stuck there.

"It's been taken care of," Wes said in an even voice.

"Good. And what was the mess with the city? You didn't tell me that, either. I swear, Wesley, you leave out all the good stuff."

"The city business has been taken care of as well."

This was the Wes I'd dealt with on the plane. I'd thought he was the real Wes, but it wasn't true. This Wes dealt with the unhappy parts of his life.

"Aren't you going to introduce us?" Jennifer Robson eyed me like a snake ready to dislocate its jaw and devour prey.

Overprotective of her son or overprotective of his assets?

"Mara, this is my mother, Jennifer." Flat tone and he stayed sitting.

I smiled and stood. I crossed over to the woman who was a couple inches shorter and stuck out my hand. "Nice to meet you."

Jennifer gave a limp shake, but her gaze could cut steel. "Mara? As in Mara Baranski? Are you the one who caused the trouble?"

Wes shot up. "Mother!"

"In fact, I am." My coat became my shield against Sam's angry ex-wife. "But as Wes said, it's been taken care of."

Jennifer wasn't going to let it go. "Why the hell would you

think that being in Sam's bed gives you the right to his fortune?"

Hypocritical much?

Jennifer squared off with her and poked her finger in my face. "Are you after Wesley now because Sam didn't work out?"

The day officially sucked.

"Back off, Mom. She came to talk to me about Sam."

"That's how women like that work," Jennifer hissed.

Wes threw his hands up. "She can be designing a custom prenup for all I care. I want some answers about why Sam cut me off after the divorce."

Jennifer drew back, her expression shuttered. "I thought we talked about how it's Sam's issue, not yours."

"I think you should tell him, Ms. Robson." My voice shook.

If I was wrong, I'd hurt someone who'd become very important to me. If I was right, Wes's world was going to get turned upside down.

Wes swung to his mom. "Tell me what?"

His mom brushed invisible dust off her couture jacket. "She's after your money."

"Mara." He towered over both of us, his expression hard.

Even on the plane, he hadn't been as close to combusting as he was now.

"Remember, I said he didn't come out and say—"

"Just tell me."

Jennifer stepped closer to her son. "She lies—"

"Quiet, Mother."

I clutched the coat tighter. "He said once he wished he hadn't walked away from you for so many reasons. Mainly because he'd ruined his only chance to be a dad. I don't—I got the impression he couldn't have kids."

I sucked in a breath and waited for Wes to figure it out.

Sam had mentioned other things that had led me to the same conclusion, but with Wes's cunning and his mom's choked expression, he'd put the pieces together.

Jennifer's chest heaved and she watched Wes with wide eyes.

"Mom?" His strangled word cut me deep, but I stayed planted in my spot, instinctively knowing he would shun my comfort.

"She's lying." Spoken with much less conviction.

"I never felt it was my place to say anything and I haven't told anyone my suspicions," I said. "I'm sorry, Wes."

"Why'd you come today?" he snarled.

His rage was understandable.

"Because you wanted to know why Sam and I got along so well. He felt like he'd lost you and I never had a dad."

"So you were the kid he never had?" Wes roared. "You were good enough, but he'd raised me and I wasn't?"

"I'm sorry, Wes," I whispered.

"Wes—" his mom cut in.

"Get out."

His mom put her hand over her heart. "Wesley."

"Not you, Mother." He glared at me, pouring all his anger into his next words. "I think it would've been better if you'd been fucking him instead. Getting to him by pretending to be the kid he'd always wanted is fucking low."

I recoiled. His words were as good as slapping me.

"Did it feel good to have the power this time, Mara? You broke up a marriage, why not break up a family?"

My arms holding the coat hung down as all the tension drained out of me. He was hurting and he had a right to. But I didn't deserve his insults or his derision. Didn't need to be showed that no matter what, he'd always see me as the greedy whore.

Wes

EVERY MUSCLE STRAINED to go after Mara. The hurt in her eyes.

"Talk."

"I never…you weren't supposed to find out." I'd never seen my mother so subdued.

My dark hair came from her. Her eyes were more hazel than blue, but they looked enough alike that I'd never questioned how different I was from Sam.

"Were you protecting me, or yourself?"

"Wesley…" She blinked back tears. Real ones.

It struck me that this was the most real moment between the two of us we'd ever had.

"He was gone so much." With a hand at her temple, she walked to the couch Mara had just been sitting on.

Out the window, Mara's car sped up my driveway.

"He moved me here." She gave a bitter laugh. "Took me away from my family, away from nice weather, and plopped me here and then was never home. I loved him. I really did. But I was lonely." She shrugged, her small smile was so sad but shockingly genuine.

"Who was he?"

"I'll give you his name, but he's married now, with other children."

Another father who wanted nothing to do with me. "Who was he?"

"Landscaper. Cliché, right? Rich wife and the gardener."

"Was he married, too?"

"No. At least I did that right. Honestly, I didn't know Sam

wasn't your biological father until you got older and you looked like…him."

I collapsed in the chair, gazing up at the ceiling. "Did you bring it up in the divorce to hurt Sam?"

Her laughter was void of humor. "I'm not that shallow. Despite what you might think. He insisted on a paternity test. I asked him why it mattered, but he had to know." She examined her fingernails, true regret etched into the fine lines on her face. "I took you in, told you it was a throat swab for strep. They were collecting the sample. I'd already told Sam I'd been cheating on him for most of our marriage, it was just confirmation. Years later, I guess he'd discovered he was infertile."

"You can leave now." I had no compunction to move. I could stare at the ceiling all day, pondering the chess pieces of my life.

"Wesley."

"Go, Mother."

She rose to her feet and her heels snapped a slow rhythm as she left the way she came.

Minutes—hell, hours had ticked by when I sat forward with a huff. I pressed my palms to my eyes, then looked around at the house. I didn't like this house, had searched for one like I'd grown up in, had thought maybe Sam would come for visits.

A glint caught my attention. Something lay on the floor between the couch and the glass end table.

I hated the furniture, too.

Retrieving the object, the emptiness within me filled with remorse. Guilt. Sadness. Loss.

The small package I held was a Wesley Crusher action figure.

CHAPTER 22

ara

"Cards are more fun with more than two people."

I laid my hand down. Mom had a point and I should tell her.

After the debacle at Wes's house, I'd been too numb to cry. I'd spent the rest of the day sorting through the leftover stock and uploading it online to sell. The funds would help me buy a new business wardrobe. If I was hired.

"I'm not seeing Sam anymore. Actually, Mom, can I tell you a story?"

Everything poured out. I started as far back as Dr. Johannsen, editing out the part where anxiety for Mom's health had distracted me. Then came Sam, the mall, Wes as Sam, Wes as Wes, and Sam as not Wes's biological dad.

Not one tear shed.

Mom's face tinted several shades throughout the tale. "Wow. Mara. I wish I could've helped."

"I didn't want to worry you."

The deep sigh of disappointment tore me apart. Not burdening Mom only gave her the impression that she couldn't even carry out the basic motherly duty of listening.

"I understand, but Mara..."

My phone buzzed. Absentmindedly, I glanced at my screen.

Wha—

I didn't cover my incredulous expression in time.

"What's wrong?" Mom asked.

"It's Wes."

"And it was Wes, who went by Sam, that treated you so horribly yesterday?" Mom's tone was carefully neutral.

"Yes."

My phone kept ringing.

"You're going to ignore him?"

We waited until my phone quit. Then it started again. With shaky hands, I shut my phone completely off.

"Are you going to be okay, Mara?" Mom's soft voice broke down the last barrier I had built.

"No, Mom." Tears welled and rolled down my cheeks. "I let him break my heart."

Wes

I STROLLED past giant brick buildings. A clash of old-style and modern gave the campus a rich appearance that spoke of its history and the promise of its future. Men and women meandered by, not a care in the world, talking excitedly about weekend plans. When had they started looking so young? My university years felt like ages ago.

Women, girls really, smiled at me. I paid them no attention. Only one reason brought me to Mara's almost alma mater.

I'd done my research, met with both Franklin, who knew my father's history with the school, and Helen, who'd taken what Mara had gone through personally. Between the three of them, they'd come up with a plan. Franklin had arranged the meeting and I had gone in search of the special guest. We'd waited until Friday afternoon after Helen had checked that Dr. Johannsen's last class of the day ended at three forty-five. I worried it'd be a freak call-in-sick occurrence but Dr. Johannsen was dedicated to his students, in so many ways.

I found the correct building and couldn't help but smile at the name etched into the plaque at the door. I located the classroom with no trouble as all the students filed out. I gave it a couple of minutes while stragglers exited and was about to turn inside when I heard a giggle. A couple strode out.

It was him. Average height, not bad looking, with sandy blond hair, ol' Jake would turn heads. Probably not enough for his taste, which was perhaps why he'd chosen a profession that gave him access to and power over vulnerable young women.

The girl, obviously a student, had a look of awe as she walked with Dr. Johannsen down the wide hallway. Most of the classrooms were empty. I tracked them to a pod of offices that occupied the end of the hallway.

Dr. Johannsen had his hand on the door handle when I flagged him down.

"Excuse me, Jake. We need to talk."

Jake narrowed his eyes in irritation. The girl viewed me with open interest, her doe eyes guileless and her clothes and hair overdone.

"I'm sorry," even Jake's voice was average, "I have a meeting with a student."

I smiled, my boardroom grin that told everyone I wasn't fucking around. "What a coincidence. It's your meeting with students I want to talk about. I'm a friend of Mara's."

Jake's eyes flared and he dropped his hand off the doorknob. He touched the girl on the elbow. "I'm sorry. We'll have to meet next week instead."

"No. You won't." My gaze stayed on Jake. "A word of advice. This guy is a sexual predator and he doesn't care about your education as much as what's between your legs."

She gasped and backed away, giving me a wide berth, then scurried off.

A flush of red crept up Jake's pasty white face. "You need to leave or I'll call campus security."

"No problem. We can talk out here while waiting for them."

Jake swore and shoved the door open. He slammed it behind me.

"What's Mara after now? She ruined my marriage and almost cost me my job."

I got comfy on a beat-up couch and tried not to think about the bodily fluids that stained it. "That's what I'd like to discuss. Why did it cost her the degree but you're still here working?"

"I was young and stupid and they understood that. I lost my *wife*."

"I'll let you in on a little secret. Wives don't like it when you fuck other women. It wasn't Mara's fault."

Jake sputtered.

"I have a task for you." I continued like I was telling Franklin what I wanted to get done for the week. "What you're going to do is approach the administration. You're going to tell them that you sabotaged Mara's grade because you knew how desperate she was. Then you'll tell them how you abused your position to take advantage of her. And here's what I expect. A diploma awarding her the business degree she rightfully earned."

"It's not going to happen."

I sat forward so abruptly, Jake jumped back. "It is and here's why. Otherwise, I will arrange for a personal audit to comb through your career, every student you've been responsible for, and I can guarantee they'll find patterns. Girls whose grades were too low to pass suddenly pulling through. Then we're going to find those girls and we're going to offer them the chance to press charges. I'll pay for their representation."

Jake clenched his teeth and balled his fists. "You're bluffing."

"I don't know if you've heard of me, but my name is Wesley Robson." I paused and watched the color drain from Jake's already pale face. Jake might not have heard of me, but he knew the last name. "Since we're sitting in Robson Hall, the building funded by my dad's generous contributions to furthering the business education of students, I'm going to guess you know that I'm not bluffing. I want this done today."

Jake almost looked relieved. "Not possible."

"Because it's Friday afternoon? It's very much possible. I've arranged it and they're waiting for you. I'll walk you there." I grinned.

CHAPTER 23

ara

IT'D BEEN two weeks since Wes had tried to call me.

I didn't get out of my car. My head rested on the steering wheel. I killed the engine but stayed in the car.

No job offers. The damn cream-colored suit I wore was on its third dry-cleaning. Maybe it was my unlucky charm.

I was only three weeks out of work with several interviews, but maybe I was rushing the process. Maybe the process didn't like a girl with nothing beyond a high school diploma. Hindsight, donkey's ass. I should've transferred to an online college and finished my degree.

Or maybe it was what I needed to email Chris. His proposal was solid and I'd need to come up with some capital, but not nearly as much as going into the venture on my own.

I could partner with Chris. I wasn't going to let men like Jake and Wes tarnish my view for the rest of my life. Wasn't going to lose myself in this stupid job search, where I was trading everything I was passionate about for dry-clean only and rush hour.

I'd constructed my reply. Digging out my phone, I pulled up the draft in my email app and sent it.

Boom. Done. Time to get out of the car and face my new world.

Freezing rain pelted the window. Snow was forecasted. Good thing I'd gotten groceries. No interviews the next day and I had Netflix. I was ready to get snowed in while everyone forgot how to drive on slick streets for a few days.

Someone tapped on my window. I yelped and flung back in the seat.

I registered my door opening and my mind reeled through how to react. Start the engine and drive away. Yank the door shut and punch the locks. Lash out.

"I'm freezing my ass off out here."

That voice. I squeezed my eyes shut.

"What are you doing here?"

"Since I don't think your phone's broken, I thought it'd work better than calling."

"No. Greedy whores don't always answer their phone."

"Come on, Mara. Look at me."

I opened one eye and glared at him through it.

Contrite Wes was not who I was expecting. Sleet peppered his face, but he didn't flinch.

"Fine." I gathered my things and got out. He closed the door behind me and ripped his J.Crew coat off to hold over me as a makeshift umbrella.

Why'd he have to go do something sweet?

I got us inside and took his coat. It didn't get hung up with my coat. I draped it over the end table next to the front door.

Right eye twitch. I counted it as a win.

He went to the couch we'd had some amazing sex on and settled in. A briefcase I hadn't noticed before rested at his feet.

I stayed standing and ordered my muscles not to fidget under his scrutiny.

"You look good. Where are you working?"

"I'm not."

"I'm sorry."

I shrugged and crossed my arms. "It is what it is."

"No, I'm sorry for the way I treated you."

"When?"

He winced. "Everything. No, I don't regret our time together, but I'm sorry for how it began. For the lies, for the insults to your character."

This conversation was going to destroy me later, but I'd hold it in until he left. Wes in my house scrambled my good sense. How right it felt shorted my *you should know better* wiring.

"Okay. You can go now."

"A few more things, please."

"Wes, I—"

He lifted the bag and grabbed some papers.

"I hate that bag," I blurted.

"I don't blame you." He held them out to me.

"No offense, but this scenario didn't go so well last time."

He set them next to him on the couch. "It's the same contract you were going to sign with Sam. I halted the demolition and the mall is yours for a dollar."

I barked out an angry laugh. Was he serious? Was this a last attempt to prove I was the greedy whore he'd always thought? I made a beeline for the papers and in front of his face, I ripped them in half. Ripped them in half again, then again, and shoved the shreds into the offensive bag.

He pressed his lips together through the whole show. "It was yours, no strings."

"Oh, there are strings, Wes. I don't want to give you my signature as proof that I'm willing to use men for personal gain."

"I don't think that," he whispered. "I've changed—"

"I've changed, too. I know better than to trust a guy who wields his power over me."

"Fair enough." He withdrew another sheet of paper.

I envisioned burning that bag in a tiny bonfire. "Oh god. What now?"

"Have a seat."

"No."

"I talked to Jake Johannsen."

The shock buckled my knees. I pivoted to land next to him on the sofa. I'd been struggling to move on and he'd been continuing his mission to ruin me. Wasn't my store enough, he had to dredge up the humiliation of my past —again?

"I'm sure his side of the story differed from mine." I couldn't look at Wes.

"Not when I told him I could arrange for his entire career to be audited."

That...wasn't what I expected to hear. "What'd you do?" I breathed.

"I did what I'm best at—wielded my power. He confessed everything." His smirk was the same one I'd seen on the plane when he'd thought he'd cornered me. "But I'm having him audited anyway."

A laugh escaped, but I sobered. "He'll just lose his job at the worst. It won't save others."

"I'm paying for the representation of any of his victims who want to take legal action."

My world slowed. Wes championing me was different

than him taking the word of women he'd never met. Paying their legal fees.

"Why would you do this?"

He adjusted until he faced me. His large, capable hands wrapped around mine and it was the first time in weeks I'd felt some of the stress of my life abate.

"I'd like to think it's because it's the right thing, but I wouldn't have known about it if it weren't for you. I want you back, Mara."

My head was shaking and I didn't realize it until he cupped my face.

"Your diploma should arrive in the next six weeks."

He grew blurry as I gazed at him through a pool of tears. Stay strong. He'd lied to me, used me, dropped me in New York, and left. But he'd held me all night when I'd needed emotional support, he'd fixed my sink, and he was championing several women he'd never met. "I've been trying so hard to hate you."

And it was hard when I'd recall how he'd pushed my mom around Comic-Con and treated her to dinner after, all while in costume. How he'd chewed me out for not accepting his private plane to get back to Minneapolis. Our laughing and silly competitions at the trampoline park. I'd wanted to hate him, but we'd had too many good times to let the hurt and lies reign supreme.

His lips touched mine briefly. "I gave up trying to hate you. Couldn't do it. Don't want to do it."

"How can I trust you again? You used me."

"I never used you," he said gruffly. "I couldn't get enough of you. But I understand. Take as long as you need, Mara, just don't shut me out. I want you in my life. I want to come home to you. I want to tell you about my day. I want you to keep showing me what love really is."

It sounded too good to be true. "No matter what, I was still friends with your dad."

"I know and I was unfair. I've thought about it a lot. Other than you, it's almost all I've thought about. I can't pretend to know how he felt, and I don't agree with what he did or my mom sending me off to school. I think she felt like she was protecting me when it just separated us more. But it happened and I can see now that he tried by teaching me how to run his business and acknowledging me in his will. And when I really thought about it, I realized, how awesome is that? You got to know him, too, and instead of being a resentful asshole, I can enjoy swapping Sam stories with you."

Speechless. Still, I tried shaking my head between his palms.

"Come back to me, Mara. There's been no one for me since the bartender first called to tell me a hot chick wanted to talk to me."

"So we *were* exclusive?" I teased with a sniffle. I gripped his wrists, my nails digging in. Too good to be true.

"One hundred percent. But I confess, I may be homeless soon."

I rubbed into his caress. A girl could get used to this. "Is there a story?"

"Only that I hated the house and I'm selling it. When you left, the emptiness was intolerable. I got it thinking Sam would approve."

Lost in the pool of his blue gaze, I stroked his wrist with my thumb. "I wasn't lying when I said how much he loved you. He called himself a coward because he couldn't crawl back, begging for forgiveness."

"Thank you for that." His voice was ragged.

We met for another kiss. He pushed me back and I let him. His weight stretched out over me was a welcome relief.

"I missed this." His lips seared a path down my neck.

Dry-cleaning number four for this suit, but if I wasn't too late for Chris's offer then it was back to leggings for me.

I worked Wes's buttons as he wrestled me out of my pants. "I missed your leggings, too."

Forget the shirt. I freed him from his trousers to direct him into me.

He laid his hand on mine that was wrapped around his erection. "That bag you hate has a new pack of protection."

"Then I won't burn it while you're sleeping."

His deep chuckle vibrated into me. Within seconds, he was positioned back between my legs. A roll of his hips and he pushed inside.

He didn't thrust right away but laid his forehead on mine. "The weather's awful. I might get snowed in."

He withdrew and pushed back in.

I moaned at the ecstasy of him stroking me. "I might make you shovel."

"I'll earn my keep."

The tightness of his body matched mine. We both tried not to rush, to savor each other.

It was no use. I arched back and exploded over him. He roared my name and shook in my embrace.

In the warmth of the aftermath, Wes held me in a grip that a tornado couldn't loosen. Mine was just as fierce.

Wes

One year later...

. . .

"I can't believe I let you talk me into this." I eyed my reflection in the mirror.

"You look amazing." Mara stood next to me and my eyes narrowed.

"I wasn't talking about me." But I rocked the Superman tights and cape, thank you very much. "It's letting people see you in that Wonder Woman costume."

She grinned and ran her hand over her purple-streaked hair. "I'm not the Amazon she was, but if it'll draw people to the booth..." She stepped back to examine me. "I think you'll definitely attract a crowd."

"I do what I can for Arcadia."

Including making Arcadia's new location the home of my *Back to the Future* pinball machine. Mara's delight when I'd showed it to her made me wish I had ten more.

"Are you sure Chris doesn't need help setting up the booth?" If I wanted to be selfish, and when it came to Mara I was, I'd admit to being grateful she'd partnered with Chris. It took some of the pressure off her, and that meant more time with me.

She had passed on my offer to help get Arcadia up and running. Her own venture, she'd said in the same breath used to refuse my dismissal of a prenup.

So fine, my team drew up a standard one to make her happy and I never planned on using it anyway.

It'd also mollified my mother, who was under strict orders to never call Mara a greedy whore again. Easy to do, since she lived in the Bahamas half the year.

"He said he'd take care of it if we tore it down at the end of the convention." Mara slipped on the yellow tiara. "He also said he'd tear it down if we could use the jet to fly to Chicago and look at a location for a second store."

"You know you don't need to ask me." I was glad to see it get use, not utilizing it much since I'd dropped my business in New York and donated the property I'd owned to the city's housing authority. Then donated the money they'd need to build affordable housing. Not completely altruistic—I no longer had the desire to travel constantly.

"It makes him feel better to offer. Were you able to recruit Flynn for Captain America?"

"Yes, after I told him that there'd be plenty of women offering to be his Betsy Ross. And then I had to tell him who Betsy Ross was."

We walked to the garage together in our new place. I'd sold the Bruce Wayne mansion, and Mara and I had settled in a place that was a quarter of the size, with no lake. But I'd kept my team of people, especially Chef.

The trip to Golden Meadows went by quickly—we'd made sure to find a place close to Wendy.

Breezing through the nursing home, we found Wendy with a smile on her face, breaking tradition and already dressed as Rey from the newest Star Wars movie. Every time we visited, I marveled at how much her color and tremors had improved. She'd never get fully better, but with the doctors Helen had found and the new treatment regimen, she wasn't deteriorating as quickly and her quality of life was vastly improved.

"Look at you two. You look amazing." Wendy used her new motorized wheelchair to start for the exit.

She called it a splurge, but to me, it was a necessity. I'd even offered to move her in, but when Mara had asked, she'd passed. Too isolating. So I spoiled the woman in any other way I could. I loved my mom in my own way, but Wendy was on a different level.

Kinda like Mara.

I grabbed Wonder Woman's hand and walked with my family outside. A family I might've never had if Sam hadn't tried to keep his memories with me alive in Mara's store. I thanked the old man every time I visited the cemetery.

As if in tune with my thoughts, and she probably was, Mara smiled up at me.

I leaned in to whisper in her ear, "I'm so going to rip that costume off with my teeth tonight."

A sultry smile curved her lips. "Funny. I was thinking the same thing."

———

FLYNN MEETS a woman who makes him use his handy skills like never before in First to Bid.

I'D LOVE to know what you thought. Please consider leaving a review for First To Lie at the retailer the book was purchased from.

FOR ALL THE LATEST NEWS, sneak peeks, quarterly short stories, and free material sign up for my newsletter.

ABOUT THE AUTHOR

Marie Johnston writes paranormal and contemporary romance and has collected several awards in both genres. Before she was a writer, she was a microbiologist. Depending on the situation, she can be oddly unconcerned about germs or weirdly phobic. She's also a licensed medical technician and has worked as a public health microbiologist and as a lab tech in hospital and clinic labs. Marie's been a volunteer EMT, a college instructor, a security guard, a phlebotomist, a hotel clerk, and a coffee pourer in a bingo hall. All fodder for a writer!! She has four kids and even more cats.

mariejohnstonwriter.com

Follow me:

ALSO BY MARIE JOHNSTON

First To Lie
First to Bid
First to Fail

CPSIA information can be obtained
at www.ICGtesting.com
Printed in the USA
BVHW071639130721
611836BV00006B/528